LAND BEYOND THE LENS

By
S. J. BYRNE

I0616935

ARMCHAIR FICTION
PO Box 4369, Medford, Oregon 97504

For more information about Armchair Books and products, visit our website at…

www.armchairfiction.com

Or email us at…

armchairfiction@yahoo.com

HIS DESTINY LAY BEYOND THE LENS

Michael Flannigan was an Earth scientist and a rocket test pilot, used to dealing with scientific facts and the language of cold, hard logic. Yet, throughout his whole life Flannigan had heard destiny calling—or singing—to him. Though he chased it to every continent on the globe, it eluded him. So then he went to the moon...

On board his spacecraft, Flannigan was plagued with dreams of a strange world and a desperate race of people. But what did these dreams mean and what, if anything, did they have to do with a world as barren and lifeless as the moon? However, with the discovery of a gigantic lens encased within a massive wall of lunar rock, Flannigan soon learned that the lens itself was a doorway—a doorway to the world of his dreams and the answer to his destiny.

FOR A SECOND COMPLETE NOVEL, TURN TO PAGE 131

CAST OF CHARACTERS

MICHAEL FLANNIGAN
This Earth scientist took a rocket ride to the moon—but he had another destiny beyond the moon…beyond the lens.

LOUISE DAREN
She was the daughter of a famed astro-physicist and Michael's beautiful fiancé—but could Michael ever truly be hers?

MNIR'SR "MNIR'RA" NIKIN'RA
Like her ancient predecessor (also the queen of her people) she, too, fell in love with a god.

DJIKN "DJIK'RI" KIN'RI
He was a strong, brave, and capable general who soon would be his people's king—if only a deceiver could be revealed in time.

ZRAND'LIR "ZRAND'RI" NZINRI
As the High Priest of Gur, he was the trusted spiritual leader of his people—yet he aspired to a loftier position.

GON'SR "GON'RI THE WARRIOR" LIT'RI
This great green brute—who despised the Seren Ni—was the most powerful leader in the history of the Bi'djar Ri.

THE SEREN NI
This peaceful race was the target of Gon'ri the Warrior's hatred—so they were obviously in need of a protector.

Whither has my lost love gone?
Altinra, she of laughter,
She whose eyes were like the dawn
Where night embraces day;
She who sings no more of me,
Who walks into eternity,
Taking only memory
Of love, like blossoms, withered...

FOREWORD

Michael Flannigan could not have told anyone when or where he first heard the words, nor could he have explained their meaning. He could not even tell if they represented a poem or a song, although his opinion inclined toward the latter. For when it did creep into his mind, once every decade or so, it came hauntingly, vaguely, as though in a language he could not define, and giving him the impression of tiny voices singing in a world that Man has never known.

It was his greatest secret—one that he had not dared share with anyone. Not even with Louise, the girl who in his normal life had won his normal affections—the affections of an ordinary man who must settle down some day and marry and raise a family, as was to be expected.

But Louise *knew*, as did her father Doctor Henry Daren, and as did many of their friends, that aside from the normal Michael Flannigan, Master of Science, electronics expert and rocket test pilot—there was another Michael Flannigan hidden away somewhere, subtly disturbing the balance of all things comprehensible.

In his childhood, she knew, he had heard the wild goose calling. The modern, stereotyped civilization in which he had tried so often to settle down had been defeated in some

5

nameless, indefinable way. It had failed to stamp him into its standard die and produce an even-humored, orthodox scientist. Whether in the physical, mental or spiritual sense, she was sure that for him there would always sound the call of distant and exotic things, of far-off places, of that adventurous beyond which lies on the other side of purple mountains and the Seventh Sea.

He would no sooner appear to settle down than he would be gone again, as though searching restlessly for a nameless thing that always taunted him, luring him relentlessly, eluding him endlessly. South America, Asia, Africa—all the farthest corners of the world failed to yield him what he sought.

She had hoped that with maturity the call would grow dim and die away and that at last she would be able to meet him on the ground she knew, but with the years his restless spirit seemed to want to burst the bounds of Earth itself. And then, when she learned that he was to accompany her father and John Deegan and Ray Gilbert on the moon trip, she felt relieved. Flannigan had wanted to go to the moon all his life. It seemed to his associates that he was actually destined to go to the moon. Perhaps that was it, she thought. Once he had achieved this ambition of his life and had returned, literally, to Earth, the wild goose would call no more.

But if she had known where the "wild goose" dwelled, she would never have let him go—if she could help it.

CHAPTER ONE
Awakening

"IF WE HIT much more of this meteor flak we'll have to give up and go home," said Daren, frowning at the radar scope.

"What's the maximum size the hull can withstand?" This was from Doctor John Deegan, the thirty-seven year-old astro-physicist, world-renowned despite his youth. A steady, even-tempered man and reliable scholar, just the type to stand up best under the strain of the responsibility, the unknown dangers, and the very close confinement of a ship that cost more than a thousand dollars for every precious pound she carried. He sat in his bunk now, bending over a collapsible plywood writing board, taking copious notes.

"I'd say up to a centimeter," said Ray Gilbert. The newspapers back on Earth were referring to him at that moment as young Doctor Raymond Gilbert, physicist, rocket specialist and ballistics expert, cheerful, capable, practical—possessing a mind that was as steady as a gyroscope. "Mean velocity is enough to give any meteors over that size sufficient mass to penetrate the hull."

"Okay," Deegan said. "Now, what is the mean velocity?"

"Roughly, that of Earth's orbital speed," Doctor Daren replied. "About eighteen miles per second. Of course, most of them are heading sunward and we're traveling toward the new moon, which puts the majority of them on our tail, and as we're hitting about ten miles per second, that still gives them an eight-mile-per-second mean velocity of impact. I wish we could stay on the moon until it's full, so that on our return trip we would enjoy the same advantage, but inasmuch as we're allowed only seventy-two hours there, we'll have to strike back in the face of this celestial flak, and the mean impact velocity against our hull will be about twenty-eight miles per second. This will reduce the minimum size and increase the danger of penetration. Putting it plainly, boys, I'd say we have only a slim chance of making it back at all. So far, we've tried not to think what would happen if a good-sized meteor hit us. Of course, radar and automatic correction helps to dodge most of the bad ones, but there are just too many meteors in outer space."

"It looks," said Deegan, "as though this first trip out here is going to be the last one for at least twenty years. More work is going to have to be done on the meteor problem. Maybe we'll have to conquer gravity, travel at lower speeds and develop super plating for the hulls."

"Whoa!" exclaimed Gilbert, flashing a smile at his companions. "For the gravity problem, tack on at least ten more years. Leave us not be visionary, chum!"

Doctor Daren did not smile. He spoke slowly and carefully, watching each man intently. "I'd say it would be at least fifty years before another man-carrying space ship will get out here," he said. "You forget that solar radiations and cosmic phenomena abound out here. Do you know what my instruments say?"

Deegan and Gilbert turned slightly pale as they stared back at the older scientist. And even Flannigan looked up from the periscope to listen.

"They say that we've bought a pretty expensive ticket for this trip, and that nobody else in the future is going to want to pay the same price." Daren's listeners knew it was costing the radiologist considerable effort to get out what he had to say.

"What is it, Henry?" asked Gilbert.

"Yes, we can take it!" put in Deegan.

Flannigan only sat there at the periscope and looked at Doctor Daren in silence.

"I want you to understand," continued the latter, "that the instruments are not mistaken. The fact is, we've already been under sufficient radiation to make us completely sterile…"

THIS WAS followed by a long moment of silence. Deegan had two children. He only frowned and thought of Gilbert, who had just gotten married, and Flannigan, who was engaged to Daren's daughter, Louise. Gilbert's mouth dropped agape in an obvious expression of chagrin, and beads of cold perspiration began to glisten on his forehead. He listened to the muffled *"ping!"* of tiny meteoric particles as they struck the outer surface of the ship, and he swallowed a great lump in his throat. Flannigan, however, was almost expressionless, except for a barely perceptible tightening of the muscles along his rugged jaws.

"Any reason for continuing onward?" asked Deegan, tonelessly.

Daren sighed, brushing kinky gray hair from his forehead, and replied, "You know the amount of government money that's gone into this expedition. We're supposed to claim the moon in the name of the United Nations. That's the principal political objective. More important still, from the scientific point of view, is my radiation research. The instruments already contain priceless information. And there is more to be gained— much more. In fact, we'll have to send remote-controlled rockets out here later with new types of instruments to pick up new stuff I'm running across that we never knew existed in outer space, or anywhere, for that matter."

"There's your answer," said Gilbert. "Let the robot ships finish the job. I'm for going back while there's still a slim chance!"

"So am I," said Deegan.

Doctor Daren raised a quizzical eyebrow and looked at Flannigan, significantly. All three men looked at Flannigan. He was not the leader of the expedition, but he was the pilot, the only member who could handle the ship reliably when it came to take-offs and landings. He was a scientist in his own right and likeable enough on the ground, but out here he had suddenly become as enigmatical as the multifaceted void of space itself. There was something about the space-flying Michael Flannigan that pointed him out as a marked man.

They could not see it in his tanned and rugged face, exactly, but under an unruly mop of jet black hair, there beneath heavy, black brows, was an unusual pair of deep blue eyes. And there it could be seen. A wildness, a desperate restlessness, an almost supernatural longing for the indefinable. At times it had camouflaged itself behind a sort of silent and defiant laughter, but now, out here on the untraveled star road to Earth's far-flung satellite, out here where the mighty Unknown assailed the sanity of the mind and breathed sheer entity into their finite, human fears, they saw that this thing in Flannigan's eyes manifested itself in an expression of determination that defied all the agencies of Man and Nature to thwart it.

Flannigan grinned humorlessly as he replied to their unspoken question, "What was it Columbus said?"

"'Sail on! Sail on!'" quoted Deegan irritably. "But Columbus had a chance, and he was only wrestling with a few thousand miles of water. We're tweaking the nose of Fate itself, Mike! Be reasonable! I say we turn back!"

"That's two votes," said Flannigan. "What do you say, Doctor Daren?"

"I am an old man," replied Daren, with a sad but eloquent smile.

"Aren't we all!" retorted Gilbert bitterly. "Let's go back! What are we waiting for?"

"For Michael Flannigan," replied Deegan, and there was ice in his tone as he glared at the dark-brewed Irishman.

NOW FLANNIGAN'S jaw muscles popped out, hard and lumpy, under a day's growth of beard. He glared at all of them, with his broad back to the control board. Large, muscular hands gripped the panel board on either side of him in an unmistakable sign of possession. He was a powerful man, fully capable of manhandling any of them.

"Listen to me," he said. "The damage to us is done. We're sterile. No kids. No family. Okay. Now we know. But we're alive—and we're out here. It's a dangerous trip. We're risking our lives every second of it. So what! Did you expect a Cook's tour? What we're doing is the most important thing in history, and half a century may pass before it is tried again. We're in communication with Earth. We can tell them what we're finding out. That information alone is worth a hundred lives. And yet we may come out of this without another scratch. So I say we're going to the moon!"

Doctor Daren might have been proud of his future son-in-law at that moment had he not been troubled by one curious impression. It was what the others felt, too, but could not explain: that Michael Flannigan wanted, more than anything in this life or any other life, to get to the moon, alive or half dead, with his companions or without them. One way or another, he had to get to the moon. Though why this was so they knew that even he could not have told them.

"Michael," said Daren. "I am the responsible leader of this expedition. Suppose I ordered you to return to Earth—*now?*"

Flannigan calmly met the menacing glare of Deegan and Gilbert. "We'd go to the moon," he answered, "and I'd risk the consequences."

Deegan stood up, clenching his fists. "That's mutiny!" he shouted.

"Not yet," put in Daren, raising his hand for silence. "I have not given him the order to return. I merely wanted to know where we stood. The fact of the matter is, I strongly recommend that we make the attempt. Let's continue onward."

Grudgingly, the two men turned back to their work. But Gilbert paused long enough to look fondly at a pinup girl on the wall beside his bunk, and his eyes grew red. It was his young wife.

Even if he did live through this, there would be no children...

FLANNIGAN slept, for the first time since their take-off twenty-four hours before. And he dreamed, but it was not a dream that belonged to mortal man.

He was Gur. In his veins flowed the god blood, and he was mighty when Earth was still young.

It was Earth of eons past, before the great cataclysm. Only the beautiful little red people and the alien green men lived there then. The spiritual, fun-loving, music-loving red ones were indigenous to Earth. They were to leave their legend behind them—tales of the little folk, of fairies and leprechauns. The race of green men had come from the stars ages before and had forgotten how to traverse the void again. These were the trouble makers, the usurpers, who made live sacrifice of the red people to their cold stone gods.

But cataclysm threatened the solar system. A large celestial body was approaching the sun, and earthquakes and deadly storms assailed the Earth. The red people and the green people turned to their gods and prayed.

Then *he* had come—Gur, Bringer of the Lens. Traveling afar in his ship, he had detected the plight of the planet Earth. He had come to its people, a giant, shining god-man of mighty powers and a superior intelligence beyond their understanding.

The sun would grow very hot, he told them. Its flames would melt the Earth and turn it into lava, and all life would be destroyed. Eons more would pass before the planet would see life again.

So he gave the red people the Lens, and they passed into it, to that other dimension and that great, endless world within, where they would be safe from the very heart of the hottest star—for the Lens was indestructible.

And the green men had come to Gur, laying down their bloodied weapons of war, saying to him that they would mend their ways and give the red men peace, if only Gur would permit them to live in the Land of the Lens.

And he had agreed, saying to them that they must obey one rule only and never break it. His single rule, given to both the red men and the green men, was that there should be peace and freedom forever. In return, they would enjoy security and eternal life, there in the hidden, secret country, the Land of the Lens. If they ever disobeyed his order, he or his son or his son's son, in future time, would return. And he would be called—the Avenger.

As the cataclysm struck, Gur, himself, entered the Lens, to sojourn for an eon or so with the peoples he had saved. While Earth softened, in the cauldron of celestial fire, into a wobbly ball of lava, the Lens remained inviolate, and life went on undisturbed within. Even when the changes occurring on Earth were so violent that a mighty piece of the planet flew away and became a satellite, bearing the Lens with it, the dwellers in the Land of the Lens knew it not. For there, on their two continents in the endless sea of their hidden world, life was secure and eternal.

Some there were who were killed by accident, on rare occasions, and infrequently a child was born, but most of the original settlers were still young when Gur prepared to leave them.

He did not wish to leave, for he had fallen in love with the fairest of the little women, queen of the red-skinned people. And she with him. Great was her sorrow in those days when she knew that Gur's time within the Lens was ended, and that for reasons she would never understand he had to travel onward in the Outer Emptiness, where the stars shone down on a new and flourishing Earth and on its cold and airless satellite, where lay the Lens.

GUR LEFT the red men in possession of one continent in that secret world and the green men in possession of the other. He reminded them again of his command regarding peace and freedom, and then he left them, to be seen no more.

But Flannigan, in his dream, saw in the hidden land, on the continent of the red men, a vast desert, a desolate wilderness filled with an endless maze of barren ridges of bluish rock, like slate. These ridges formed unscalable walls, and anyone losing his way there would be lost forever. It was here the red men came when they had tired of twice ten thousand years or more of life. This was the Walk Alone that led to eternal sleep. And here he saw Gur's loved one, the saddened queen of the red ones. It was she who walked there, alone. And he heard, not in his own mind, but in Gur's, the sound of tiny voices singing for him his own lament:

> *Whither has my lost love gone?*
> *Altinra, she of laughter,*
> *She whose eyes were like the dawn*
> *Where night embraces day;*
> *She who sings no more of me,*
> *Who walks into Eternity,*
> *Taking only memory*
> *Of love, like blossoms, withered...*

Flannigan awoke with a start, to find Daren wiping his face with a sterile towel from the first-aid chest. Deegan and Gilbert, pale-faced and bewhiskered, were looking over his shoulder in amazement.

"Good Lord, Michael!" exclaimed the elderly scientist. "You're perspiring enough to dissolve! What kind of nightmare was that? You've been muttering and groaning to yourself for hours!"

Flannigan sat up, staring at his companions wide-eyed, like a madman.

"There's more!" he cried out in desperation, thinking of the song he had heard. "There's another part to it!"

"To what? Your dream? What was it?"

Flannigan shook his head to clear it. "I—I guess it was a dream," he said. "I'm going space batty."

Gilbert smiled wryly. "You have company," he said. "And we still have thirty-six hours to go!"

CHAPTER TWO
The Bell of Urg

AFTER HIS strange, disturbing dream, Flannigan remained silent, and his companions left him alone with his thoughts—and the periscope. He spent his time observing the moon, which now looked as large as the iridescent Earth astern. He knew that the ballistics called for a landing in the southern part of Mare Serenitatis, but he also knew that that was the wrong place for him. Somewhere in that barren world—*the Lens was calling.* But where?

It was late in the second day out that the meteor struck. The radar compensator could not handle the cloud they were traversing, and an iron fragment the size of a ping-pong ball neatly penetrated the hull. Air began to shriek away through two holes, one on either side of the single cabin the men occupied. But they had come prepared. Within five seconds they had rubberized emergency patches over the holes, and the internal air pressure held them in place. Spiny fingers of frost sprang into place around the patches where moisture in the air contacted the deep cold of outer space, while the battered ship hurtled soundlessly onward.

Without saying a word, they set to work and welded small patches of sheet steel over the holes. Then Gilbert turned on Doctor Daren. His face was pasty white.

"Let's turn back!" he demanded. "I've had enough!"

"So have I," put in Deegan. "Let's get out of here! There's a lot more of this stuff out here, and you know that if we get back at all it'll be a miracle!"

Daren nodded in quiet assent. "We are fortunate," he said, "that no one was cut through by that meteor. I think it is best to return. Flannigan?"

Flannigan looked up slowly from his instruments and turned around to face them. His big hands swatted his knees with a resounding "*smack!*" His eyes bored into Daren's.

"No," he said, in an even voice. But it was emphatic.

Daren's face hardened. "I am in command here," he said. "You will change course for home!"

"No."

In that moment, Gilbert managed to bring into play the wrench he had been hiding. It struck Flannigan heavily on the forehead. The Irishman's eyes closed and he fell to the floor, while dark blood poured out of the ugly gash between his dark brows.

There was no time for remorse. The other two men knew Gilbert had not intended to kill him. But violent action had been justified, because Flannigan had mutinied.

"Do you think you can pilot us?" Deegan asked Gilbert, after Flannigan's body had been pulled to one side.

"I'll have to. But it'll take hours to decelerate enough to turn around. With our extra fuel we won't have to contact Earth Base for ballistics."

"All right," said Daren, "but get on with it!" His face was a mask of pain and regret as he looked down at Flannigan's prostrate form...

BUT FLANNIGAN was not dead. He was unconscious, while his mind wandered afar. And once again he heard those elfin voices singing an epic song:

Where wanders Jith'loor now,
The joyful king, our ruler, gone, of old?
Where goeth he, with Ank'torna,
Beloved queen, his lover,
—tale untold!

Who stilled the silver flute song
Of Rah'doorjeen the Player
from our heart?
Who knelled to him the Death Song
At Eve of Tears and made him
from us depart?

No more the myriad children
Of Life and Love and Laughter
we shall behold
On Mag'dur's peak or Kild'rn,
On flowered plain of Raj'dur
—they're dead and cold!

Flannigan felt himself drawn by the strange lament through space and time, into the far-off hidden land...

DJIK'RI HELD his strong spear arm ready, and he poised his *kimblor*-wood shield expertly. He waited calmly for the vicious charge of the Zat, for it was fully aware of his presence. Had he not splattered a *d'nkun'ror* fruit all over its ugly, four-fanged snout? No warrior-hunter of Serin-Gor would have dared to hunt the swift, eight-legged

Zat alone other than Djikn Kinri, of whom the bards of the land were already composing songs for coming eons of time.

He grinned excitedly as his keen eyes met those of the Zat. It had crept aggressively forward on the forest path, searching him out for its legitimate supper. Its hairy face and mad red eyes were made the more horrible by a great, slavering mouth held perpetually agape by saber-like tusk-fangs.

Suddenly, it shrieked like an insane man and ran like the wind on its spidery legs straight down upon its smaller adversary. But Djik'ri did not give one inch of ground. His greatest weapon was fearlessness, and since the Zat depended upon freezing its victim with terror, it found itself vulnerable to this unexpected technique.

Djik'ri merely transfixed the beast with his spear and stepped to one side as it died in a bloody frenzy of unvented rage.

The young hunter smiled serenely at the size of his specimen. Even though Djik'ri was taller and stronger than most of his fellow Serin Ni, it made little difference in this case. The single-handed killing of this giant Zat proved that he was a mighty hunter. But Djik'ri wanted most of all to convince himself of his prowess. Let others think what they would. He was soon to reach maturity and he had important plans, brave and daring plans which might one day shake this whole world of Gra'ghr.

He turned and looked happily out over the flowered plain of Raj'dur, down from the forested slopes of Mag'dur, and out upon the glistening white, stone city of Rurz'tlid and to the blue expanse beyond, which he knew was Ces'son Nar—the Barrier Sea. He drew up the full one-foot-and-nine-inches of his athletic frame, patted the red skin of his stomach and swelled out his chest. Ah, but it was good to be alive in this beautiful world! This night he would send a prayer to Gur, thanking him for all the wonders of life that were his to enjoy!

Suddenly, there rolled up to him out of the city a very discordant sound, Djik'ri knew that terrible sound too well, but he tried almost with a superhuman effort of the will to convince himself that he had not heard it.

"No! Lord God Gur!" he shouted to the sky in sudden sorrow. "Let not the black Bell of Urg toll forth!"

But in a moment he heard the sound again, and no longer could he deny that Urg had come. The dreaded sound rolled over the countryside like a tidal wave, drowning the spirit of life and hope.

Sadly, Djik'ri wiped off his spear and prepared to go home, even forgetting the tremendous Zat he had killed. He was thinking of his people and their heavy hearts at the sound of the Bell of Urg. And he thought of his sister, Mnir'sr Nikin'ra, queen ruler of Serin-Gor. She in particular would suffer the depths of sorrow. He must comfort her.

Accursed Urg! One day he, Djikn Kinri the Hunter, Son of Jith'loor, would end this law of the ages, and Urg would be no more... As he walked down the hunting road, through the colorful plain of Raj'dur, his greenish-blue hair waved in the wind, and his ink-black eyes glared defiantly at the temple tower from which had knelled the mournful announcement that Urg, the Season of Death, had begun...

MNIR'SR NIKIN'RA the Queen, known to all her devoted friends and subjects as Mnir'ra, laughed like a happy child. The gaseous *ntik'a* water boiled about her like a dazzling cloud of pearls in the bright yellow light of the four suns of Gra'ghr. It warmed her naked body and buoyed her up and tickled her all at the same time as she was carried down the rapids in a race with Djur Djinri the Swimmer.

All of the people of Serin-Gor were born swimmers, but they swam best of all in the warm, bubbling spring waters of the River Toor, which passed through the bright city of Rurz'tlid. And never were they so enthusiastic as when their young queen took part in their sports. Naked and beautifully this red people swam, strong men and graceful women, innocent of shame, deserving tenants of the paradise in which they lived.

"Mnir'ra tied Djur'ri!" cried a chorus of young men and women at the end of the race, where the river turned toward the sea. The contestants sprawled all about on great, warm, white rocks near the arched stone bridge that led to the palace. A dozen eager hands reached out to help their beloved ruler out of the water.

Mnir'ra laughed in triumph at having tied Djur'ri, the champion, in the race. And she laughed for the sheer joy of living, a joy which was enhanced, perhaps, by the realization that hers was the greatest beauty in the land. Her delicate skin was not as reddish as that of most of the girls, but rather an inimitable shell-pink color. Her hair was the purest blue of the sea, reaching down almost to her waist.

Her maids threw a great white robe about her shapely shoulders and began to comb and brush her voluminous hair as she sang to all who were within range of the clear fairy piping that was her voice. Mnir'ra the Singer began to sing the Song of Life:

We sing to Life, our eyes look up,
Alight with joy and laughter.
There is no strife, we fill our cup,
Today and ever after,

Our joyous call of life and love
Through endlessness goes ringing
To purple Ral, swift moon above,
Who hears our people singing.

"Who hears our people singing!" chorused her listeners.

Boom-m-m!

The singing stopped.

Boom-m-m!

Joyous faces turned pale and all eyes looked up river at the great temple tower.

Boom-m-m!

"The Bell of Urg!" cried Djur'ri sorrowfully.

"Oh, hateful Urg!" cried others. "How surely does Urg cast its shadow on the path of light!" "It is a thing accursed!" "It should never be!"

All began to cover their graceful forms with their bathing robes and excuse themselves from the young Queen's presence. Sadness had leapt upon them like a deadly, nocturnal Kran'jandoon, enmeshing them in its writhing, inescapable web. The shadow of death was to lie upon the land of Serin-Gor for six purple moons.

QUEEN MNIR'SR NIKIN'RA said nothing after that. The knelling of the black Bell of Urg continued from the temple while she walked in sorrow back to the palace. There she was dressed in the mourning robes of the Urg season, and she soon retired to the gardens to walk alone with her thoughts.

She cried bitterly in protest against the Law of Urg. While she sat by the great fountain of the palace garden and wept, some of the royal bards, playing their stringed instruments atop the palace towers, faced the lowering suns and began to sing the traditional Song of Urg.

The sad, elfin, trembling notes of their instruments, the tearful singing of the bards, and the vivid realization of the sorrowful task before her, because of the Law of Urg, made Mnir'ra sob as though her heart would break.

She must, within six purple moons, herself select one hundred youths and one hundred maidens, to be made ready for the ships of the green men, the powerful and ferocious Bi'djar Ri from across the Barrier Sea. These youths were not of the eternal stock who had lived beyond the reckoning of memory. They had to be like herself and her brother Djik'ri—new born and just coming to maturity, or just arrived to it. They would be sacrificed to the bloody stone gods of the green men.

Her mind dwelled in bitterness upon the clever treachery of her enemy. The ancient command of Gur, Bringer of the Lens, had been that there should endure peace and freedom forever, between red men and green men alike. Or else the Son of Gur, the Avenger, would come back through the Lens. She doubted that the green men still believed in the old legends. In fact, most of her own people seemed to regard the ancient tale of the Lens as a children's story. Yet Mnir'ra saw in the plan of the green men a clever loophole, should the Avenger ever really come. For under the Law of Urg, established by mutual agreement between the red-skinned Serin Ni and the green-skinned Bi'djar Ri, peace and freedom still remained, though in name only. In ages past, the Bi'djar Ri had threatened to invade the land of Serin-Gor unless the red men agreed to supply them, at precise intervals, with victims for their sacrifices. This, they said, would serve to keep the peace, and the Serin Ni would maintain their freedom.

Mnir'ra reflected that if the priests of the red men of Gur had had real faith in the promise of their god that he or his son or his son's son would return, in case of war, the Law of Urg would never have been established. But they had been of little faith in those days, as they were now, and they had feared the green men. And so the Law of Urg became fixed in the pattern of their existence. Every hundred purple moons the Bell of Urg knelled forth its call of death in the land of Serin-Gor.

The Law of Urg had become an ancient and unbreakable pact. It called for hideous tribute, payment in life's precious blood, for the privilege of not being invaded. And in these times the law was more rigidly enforced than ever before, by Gon'sr Lit'ri, the present ruler of the Bi'djar Ri. In fact, some suspected that one day this famous Gon'ri the Warrior, as he was called, would break the pact and conquer Serin-Gor anyway. For he, of them all, believed nothing of the old legends. He believed only in appeasing the hungry gods of his own land.

But life under him would be without happiness of any kind, and the sacrifices would not only continue. They would increase without limitations. As long as he did not break the pact, therefore, the tribute required by the Law of Urg was the lesser of the two evils, but it almost strangled Mnir'ra's compassionate heart to contemplate her dreaded responsibility as ruler of the land, during the Season of Urg.

"It is sad," said a deep voice beside her, "that you know nothing of the art of rationalizing, Queen Mnir'ra."

MNIR'RA turned her tearful face upward to look into the cold eyes of Zrand'lir Nzinri, High Priest of Gur. He was almost as tall as her brother, Djik'ri, but he had a lean and hungry look about him which reminded her more of the Season of Urg than of the Hundred Moons of Life which came between. Always during the Season of Urg, Zrand'ri seemed to take more interest in his job than at any other time. He it was who always rang the black Bell of Urg when the hundredth purple moon had set.

"What must be must be," he told her. "Can you not control your mind sufficiently to accept facts as they are? It is such folly to subject yourself each time to these rebellious emotions! As Queen you should be strong and uphold the Law of Urg, as did your father, Jith'loor, and your queen mother before you. Tomorrow you must prepare the lots which shall be drawn."

Little Queen Mnir'ra sat up and tried to dry her eyes, but more tears flooded out upon the others. "May Gur have mercy on me!" she cried. "But I curse the Law of Urg! It is not a way to keep the ancient commandment! It is sacrilege! I can think nothing else of you, Zrand'ri, than as a worshipper of the heartless gods of the Bi'djar Ri, so zealously do you seek to gather their innocent victims!"

Zrand'ri darkened visibly at this. He straightened up, tall and forbidding in his black robe, and he glared down upon Mnir'ra in righteous wrath. He even raised his hand to strike her, but then hesitated, mindful of the palace guards who were fanatic about their queen.

"Who speaks of sacrilege!" he cried out. "What horror of words is this from the mouth of a queen! You must come to the temple and pray to Gur to erase those words from the Book of Judgment, where they have surely been written against you!"

"If I pray at the temple, or anywhere else," cried Mnir'ra, "it will be to ask Gur to lift from this land the curse of Urg!"

Zrand'ri decided to change his tactics. He calmed down and appeared to reason with her. "But do you not love this fair land? Surely you would not want Gon'ri the Warrior to invade it and lay it waste and make of us a nation of slaves!"

"No!" cried Mnir'ra, helplessly.

"But someday Serin-Gor must grow strong enough to overthrow the Bi'djar Ri, and then—"

"That day will never come," smiled Zrand'ri, amused. "You are children of play and song and dancing. You know naught of industry and progress. Else by now you would have great ships to cross the sea, and metal bows for your arrow, to fight back at those who come to take the toll of Urg!"

Mnir'ra could not deny the superiority in strength of her despised enemy. Nor could she guess what means might be used to overcome him.

"You should be sensible and do what is your duty," argued the High Priest of Gur. But he was thinking more than he expressed in words.

No one in all the land of Serin-Gor knew the secret thoughts of Zrand'ri, probably because they could not imagine such deception. Zand'ri, too, was tired of Urg, but not because it pained him to see the land deprived of youths and maidens. It was because he longed for power over the land. He, Zrand'ri, wished to be king in place of Djikn Kinri, who was soon to reach maturity and acquire the throne from his sister. And he had already entered into a secret plan that had been found attractive to Gon'ri the Warrior-a plan which might gain support from the green man ruler in acquiring for Zrand'ri the throne of Serin-Gor...

"Good day, my queen," said the priest, suddenly, for he had seen the striding figure of Djik'ri the Hunter enter the garden gate from the palace. He desired as little conversation as possible with that hot-headed upstart. Hurriedly, he walked toward a side entrance to the garden.

MNIR'RA looked up at her brother with a sad but welcoming smile. She stretched out her hand to him and pressed his own hand firmly.

"Dear Djik'ri," she said, "the sight of you is my only consolation in this dark time. I need you so!"

Djik'ri laid a hard, muscular hand on the fine blue hair of her head and stroked it fondly. He had asked her as a favor to him never to cut it, and now it lay down her back, a sea of loveliness.

"Poor Mnir'ra," he said. "I want to help you. Ever since the Bell of Urg began to toll I have been thinking of many things. You know, today I killed a giant Zat."

Mnir'ra looked up at him quickly, her brow furrowed with concern. "Ah, Djik'ri, how often have I begged you not to risk your life like that! Why do you do it?"

Djik'ri looked sternly at her. "Because I must prove my strength," he said. "Do you recall what accursed day is my birthday?"

"It was a *blessed* day when you were born, my brother!" she protested, kissing his hand in an outburst of affection.

"You know it is the Day of Urg, on which the sacrifice victims must depart on the ships of the Bi'djar Ri. But *this*

Day of Urg, six purple moons from now, I shall be of age! What does that mean to you?"

"Thank Gur, you will be king, Djik'ri!"

"And from that moment on I shall prepare this land to fight the green men and rid the world of the Law of Urg!"

"But that will bring only war and bloodshed and defeat for all of us, my brother! How can you hope to fight the green men who have strong metal bows and great ships of sail?"

Djik'ri's fists clenched and his jaws tightened. "Somehow, I shall find a way," he said bitterly.

From the palace roof, while the four suns of Gra'ghr went down beyond Ces'son Nar, the bards still sang the endless Song of Urg, which went on day and night throughout the Season of Urg:

Fair Nil'ra hears us crying,
She hears the mir'h trees sighing
'neath Purple Moon.
O ancient Queen of Beauty,
Thy love-path in the woodland
was left too soon!

No more your sandaled footsteps
Tread light the hills of Rurz'tlid,
where r'ur birds cried.
You sleep where Yuh'dlir slept
In caves of dread; where Jin'r hid
and our hearts died!

"Djik'ri," said Mnir'ra softly.

"Yes?" Djik'ri had been carried away by racial memories which the wailing Song of Urg engendered in his mind.

29

"Let us go up and pray to Gur."

"For what?"

"Have you no faith, then, Djik'ri?"

Djik'ri looked sullenly at the ground. "Faith?" he said. "I sometimes wonder at a god that would accept Zrand'ri as his priest."

"Djik'ri! Do not say that! I hold with you that Zrand'ri is not good, but I, for one, still firmly believe in the ancient legend of the Lens. Remember, Gur's promise was that, if peace and freedom were disturbed, he or his son or his son's son would return, and he would be called the Avenger. If we have genuine faith, then all we have to do is reject the Law of Urg. If Gon'ri attacks, his very act of aggression will bring us the Avenger!"

DJIK'RI STUDIED his sister for a good long while. Then he said, "Would that I might share this faith with you. But I can do one thing! I can match your faith with an army. Then, if the Son of Gur fulfills the ancient promise, he will have us as his loyal allies, to fight by his side. If he does not come—there will still be the army, and *me!*"

Mnir'ra laid her hand on her brother's arm. "Have faith, Djik'ri. Let us ask Gur to deliver us all from the curse of Urg!"

"Then let Gur give us a sign, a thing that I may see with my eyes! Come! I have a prayer for Gur myself!"

On the roof of the palace, in a section removed from the players and singers of the endless Song of Urg, Mnir'ra and Djik'ri lighted holy fires to Gur, and Mnir'ra said her prayer first:

"Great Gur, hail to thee, O Bringer of the Lens! Hear me, Mnir'ra, distant daughter of thy sacred love of old,

Altinra, she who walked alone in Zi'ilgar-Lon, the Desert of Death, to mourn thy absence and to seek eternal sleep! Now her faith is born anew in me, and I am thy humble servant who bows before thy eternal wisdom and humbly begs thy indulgence in this dark hour of sorrow and despair. Grant us, O shining God of eons past, that our people will never more set foot upon the ships of the Bi'djar Ri to die in sacrifice to the false gods of our enemy! Return, O Gur of our fathers, or send us Gurund Ritroon—Son of Gur, the Avenger—to win us justice and safety from our dreaded enemy and enable the people of Serin-Gor to live in peace and freedom and happiness forever!"

Almost expectantly, Mnir'ra raised her face toward the heavens, where now only Lan Ba'na, the golden moon, pursued her departed brother, Ral, through the starless sky of Gra'ghr. Djik'ri, too, looked for some sign of response to the prayer.

Then, as a king might speak, he looked up at the sky and said, "Great Gur, soon I shall be king. I have made myself strong, O Gur, and it is in my heart to make my people strong to fight against the wild armies of Gon'ri the Warrior. Give me, therefore, some sign that thou wilt put thy strength behind me! Lend thy great hand to this cause, O mighty Gur!"

Again, both worshippers looked expectantly at the sky. But again they saw nothing but Lan Ba'na, the golden moon. After a while, Djik'ri frowned angrily at the sacred fires.

"There is no god," he said, "nor are those fires sacred. It is all but sham and illusion. We are alone upon this globe, and the battle is ours to fight alone."

Mnir'ra suddenly stood up and gripped her brother's shoulder. He looked at her and found her pointing in amazement toward a distant point which lay beyond the dark shoulder of Mag'dur.

"We have been looking in the wrong direction!" she exclaimed. "We forgot the *ancient* temples, where Gur once truly lived! There is a light, Djik'ri! Look!"

Djik'ri looked, and then he became speechless with wonder. For there where he knew the incredibly ancient ruins of the temples to be, he saw vague tendrils of white light reaching upward into darkness.

"There is your sign!" cried Mnir'ra. "It is a signal to us! A call!"

Djik'ri looked unblinkingly at the weird lights in the distance, until they faded suddenly into a veil of darkness again.

"I must follow that sign," he said, "to prove that it was not some useless hallucination. It must yield a definite symbol or message to me from Gur, and if it be so then I shall take great courage and have great strength as king. Mnir'ra, I must go at once!"

"Take me with you!" she pleaded, excitedly, not fully realizing what strange things were stirring in her breast. "I, too, must see this miracle, for I feel that the ancient power of the Lens is awakening!"

"Then follow me!"

NONE THERE were who saw the yellow-haired, gryphon-like Ban'thorn with its hawkish head which carried Djik'ri and his sister swiftly on its silent paws across the rising plain of Raj'dur, under the bright rays of Lan Ba'na, the golden moon of Gra'ghr.

They rode afar, for the ancient temple ruins lay beyond the shoulder of Mag'dur. They rode onward through the night, deep into wilderness, searching desperately for a physical proof of the great miracle for which they had prayed...

CHAPTER THREE
Into the Lens

GILBERT instructed his two companions to tie themselves into their bunks in preparation for heavy deceleration. Flannigan's body had been picked up off the floor and placed in his own bunk. They had strapped it down extra tight.

As the deceleration, increased, the blood drained from their faces and their flesh pressed against their skulls so that the face of each man looked like a shining death's head. Daren blacked out first, then Deegan. But Gilbert clenched his teeth until he thought he had welded his jaws together forever, and he struggled to peer out of an encroaching blackness, while his tense, white fingers clutched the remote control beside him which activated the decelerator feed-valves.

He was reflecting, dimly, that a man might weigh about fourteen hundred pounds now if he could be put on a scale. Then, suddenly, he thought he was losing his mind, for out of the corner of his eye he saw Flannigan's form move! He could barely turn his head, but when he finally did he saw Flannigan staring at him through the caked blood that half covered his face! Gilbert knew when he saw the hideous, open gash splitting Flannigan's forehead, that the man would be scarred for life, if he lived to see the Earth again.

There was a loud report, as though someone had fired a gun in the room, and Flannigan sat up between broken safety straps. Gilbert froze with terror, for this was supernatural! Either that or he was out of his mind and suffering delirium tremens.

Now Flannigan unloosened his remaining straps and stood up, where no human being could possibly stand. Except for the half-mask of blood on his face, he was colorless, almost white as marble, and he glistened with perspiration. Slowly, as though Gilbert were seeing him in the unreality of a dream, he crossed the room and removed Gilbert's fingers from the remote control. His hand seemed cold.

Within a few seconds, the deceleration was stopped, and color began to come back into everyone's faces, all except Flannigan's. Daren and Deegan came to and looked in uncomprehending amazement at their pilot.

"He's inhuman!" screamed Gilbert hysterically. "He broke his straps and stood up! He just walked over and took control!"

"Flannigan!" said Daren peremptorily.

But Flannigan kept his eyes glued to the periscope. It was as though he were unaware of their existence.

Deegan rose silently to his feet and made a sign to Daren and Gilbert. Slowly, tensely, the three of them got together in the middle of the room, shoulder to shoulder. And then they sprang upon the Irishman.

Headlocks, arm locks, rabbit punches and mad, desperate lunges and tuggings all proved to be of no avail. Flannigan merely turned around and flung them to the opposite end of the control room. They lay panting in the spell of a nameless fear, for they had felt in their opponent an irresistible strength that was alien to their kind.

His strange, deep blue eyes stared at them in such a way that they could not endure it, and they turned their faces, only to look back again in horrified fascination.

"Flannigan!" gasped Daren from his spot on the floor. "What in the name of Heaven has come over you? You are taking us all to our deaths! You know that! We've got to turn around! Go back, Flannigan! Go back!"

"It is said that God created the Universe," said Flannigan, in a rumbling, stentorian tone they had never heard before. "But there are other universes—and my own destiny would be incomprehensible to you. So you shall do as I say, until we get to the moon. After that, the ship is yours. I can explain no more."

THEY DID not land in Mare Serenitatis. Flannigan had seen, at last, what he knew he had been looking for all his life, yet he was sure no human eyes could have discerned the eerie tendrils of light reaching out into space toward the tiny rocket. Ghostly hands of an ancient power, calling the Wanderer home...

Beyond Serenitatis they hurtled, close now, so close that the chalk white, towering walls of the lunar Appenines swept past within twenty miles. Lower still, hurtling across Eratosthenes and onward toward the fifty-mile crater of Copernicus, almost to the ageless shore of Mare Imbrium. Then, a blood-draining turn, and they were coming down, stern first, alongside the Earth-illuminated walls of the crater Rheingold.

After the landing had been secured, Daren said, "We are the first men on the moon, Flannigan. I don't know what your plans are, but now that we're here we'll have to communicate with Earth Base concerning our new position and the ballistics for take-off. I believe they'll still make us wait here the planned seventy-two hours. In view of this I'd like to continue as planned and make our explorations and tests."

"I said that when we reached the moon the ship would be yours," Flannigan replied. He was already entering the hatch to go below to the space suits and the airlock.

But Daren detained him, trying to find some trace of the old Flannigan in those cold blue eyes. "Where are you going?" he said. He, too, noticed the ghastly wound on the other's forehead and knew it would leave an indelible scar.

Flannigan looked at him with that piercing, alien look that was so hard to endure. "I go where no man may tread," he answered. "So don't try to follow me."

Daren looked at Deegan and Gilbert and saw that they were as helpless as he was to detain the other. Then he looked back into the alien blue eyes.

"We have just seventy-two hours, Flannigan," he said. "Maybe less."

"Don't look for me."

Daren's fingers gripped Flannigan's shoulder, hard. "Don't be a fool, man! What about returning to Earth—to Louise!"

Just for a fleeting instant, Flannigan's eyes softened. Then he said, "I am sterile."

"Is that why you're determined to commit suicide?"

"This is far from suicide. It is an awakening—and a duty. Goodbye!"

"Then we'll have to return without you?" Daren called through the hatch.

But Flannigan was already getting into his space suit...

UNDER THE bright, bluish-white light of the Earth, the moon lay cold and terribly silent, its jagged mountains and crater walls looking like the jumbled ruins of a city of Titans-now resentful of being disturbed out of its sleep of ages. Flannigan, under his armor plate hood and back shield, was climbing the jagged wall of Rheingold. Once in a while, a tiny meteoric particle pinged against his hood, but outside of that he was surrounded by the cloying, almost tangible stillness of interplanetary space. He paused only once to look back at the ship. It lay over a mile below him, a tiny, dim spot of Earth-light reflection. Daren and the others, he reflected, must have claimed the moon already in the name of the United Nations.

He looked upward also at the looming face of Earth— the planet that had borne his flesh out not his spirit. The part of him that was a man turned fleetingly to earthly memories—white gulls gliding on the tangy air over the small blue bay of Mazatlán, colored sails in the sunset off Waikiki, the blinding whiteness of eternal snow mantling the Andean horizon across lofty Titicaca, the multi-laned traffic at Wilshire and Western in Los Angeles, the misty panorama of San Fernando Valley in the early morning, the smell of fresh coffee, the warm breath and the soft lips of a blonde, blue-eyed girl—Louise. Perhaps—no, he was quite sure of it—he would never see these things again. Beyond Earth, the unblinking abyss of stars was like the raven, saying, "Nevermore!"

He turned his face again, abruptly, toward the rim of Rheingold, beyond which dawned a corona of writhing light which he knew was not being registered by his eyes of flesh and blood. There was an older eye, and an older blood—and these were responding now to the call of the Lens, with a will that was his own and yet not his own, but which he had to admit was superhuman.

Even in the midst of it all, Flannigan, the man, had to ask himself: What is a god supposed to do? Because he knew that such he would be in the Land of the Lens. An ancient destiny, written on the sands of time that were buried under a thousand strata before the birth of Man, had made it so...

Three hours later, Flannigan entered a crevasse that split the inner wall of Rheingold. He followed the natural floor, wading ankle deep in cosmic dust that rose and fell with peculiar abruptness, having no air to support it. In his tanks there was air however. Enough for three days. Under the light lunar gravity he was carrying six hundred Earth pounds of equipment.

There beneath the lunar surface, in a low-roofed cavern, he found the Lens. He could only guess at its dimensions, because it glowed now with a light that was detectable even to his physical vision, and it half blinded him. He could only make out that it was half imbedded in a wall of frozen lava, a wall that had once been boiling liquid in the unimaginable heat of solar disruption, but which could never affect the alien substance of the Lens.

As he approached it, his steps faltered, and finally he stumbled and fell to the ground, his senses reeling. A million fish-hooks, it seemed, were plucking the flesh from his bones—and a cosmic force hurled him into vastness, where the Maelstrom of Creation spun him into vertigo. He felt finite and infinite. Instantaneous and eternal, occupying nothing and yet filling all time and all space, while an incomprehensible sound, the almost undetectable diminuendo and the unendurable crescendo and crashing of the music of the spheres, assailed him and fanned the forces of his life into a flame that consumed the finite man and forged a new being: a godling, drifting down paths not traversed for eons, into a far-off place, a secret land—the hidden Land of the Lens...

HE AWOKE to the sound of wild birds singing, and through his mind ran the words of a song he had heard before:

> *No more your sandaled footsteps*
> *Tread light the hills of Rurz'tlid*
> *when r'ur birds cry...*

And he knew these were the *r'ur* birds. He knew that the wind he heard was sighing in the purple-flowered *mir'h* trees that stood about among the towering walls of the ancient temple ruins. For this was Serin-Gor, and Djik'ri the Hunter and Mnir'ra the Singer were coming to him here in the wilderness to bid him welcome. They would be riding a gryphon-headed Ban'thorn, hastening to find him and serve him, for he was Gurund Ritroon—Son of Gur—the Avenger.

He knew what had brought him here. He understood the trouble that was in the land, and he knew who would be his friends and who would be his enemies. Chief among these latter were Zrand'ri, the false High Priest of Gur, and across dark Ces'son Nar, the Barrier Sea, lay Bi'djar-Tan, land of the green men, home of Gon'ri the Warrior, who was an unbeliever, a would-be conqueror standing at the head of unnumbered, battle-hungry men, plotting to defy the ancient commandment, to destroy the peace and freedom established by his father, of old. Here there was work to do.

But first of all, Gurund Ritroon was hungry. He shook his head to clear it of dizziness, and then he got to his feet.

He was naked, but that could wait. His people, the Serin-Ni, would clothe him. In the meantime, a skirt of *kimblor* bark would suffice.

So in the dawn light of the four suns of Gra'ghr he walked naked into the forest in search of food. He had not gone far before he was confronted by a hideous eight-legged creature that was half again his own size. It had an ugly, four-fanged snout, and when it charged him it shrieked like an insane man.

The Zat pounced upon its strange, white prey and caught the large man-thing's muscular arm between its powerful jaws. But the man-thing took it by the mouth and easily tore its jaws apart. As it died, it realized, vaguely and too late, that this was no man-creature of Serin-Gor. It was the mightiest being in the world...

Later, when Gurund Ritroon stepped out of the forest to look at the wild shoreline of Ces'son Nar, where lay the great temple ruins, he wore a skirt of scarlet *kimblor* bark. And he was not hungry any more. Only thirsty.

He stood on the edge of a low bluff, above rock-strewn sand, and he sniffed the air. Somewhere in the depths of his mind a memory stirred, of another place which someone attached to his past had known in the days of his childhood. A green, peaceful place called Kilarney. This place reminded him of it. This was the magical place, the hidden land of the tiny folk—the leprechauns—this other-world memory seemed to tell him. But he was small now, himself, whereas in that other life he had been large. Even so, he knew he was a head taller than the red people, and all the strength of that other-world man, plus some the Lens had added, was concentrated in his small, densified frame. That was why the Zat's teeth had only scratched him lightly, and that is why he had been able to tear it apart.

He passed his hand over his forehead. He expected to find an open wound there, but there was none. Whatever had been the injuries, defects or weaknesses of that other self, they had been obliterated by the Lens. He was reborn.

TO HIS LEFT was a small waterfall. He leapt to the beach below him and approached it. Something stirred within his spirit as he walked. He did not know what mysterious thing it was, but he sensed that it was good. Perhaps it was the sweetness of the scented air, or his sense of terrible strength and well-being—or an awareness of achievement, of something he had wanted to accomplish for millennia of time. Maybe that was it. He had arrived at last to search for his lost love Altinra, or was it his father's love, or someone else in whom the memory of Altinra had been born again?

When he drank from a great, clear pool at the foot of the waterfall and saw bright, silvery fish swim toward a cool-green, sandy bottom, he felt better than ever.

Then, suddenly, when he looked up, he saw them. They were seated on the Ban'thorn, on the opposite side of the pool. The weird beast stared fixedly at him with baleful yellow-green eyes.

On its back sat Djik'ri, a handsomely built little fellow. His skin was reddish; his hair, which touched his muscular shoulders, was of a glistening blue-green color; and his fearless but somewhat amazed eyes were coal black. He wore trunks and sandals, and on his back was a large quiver which contained three long spears. At his side was a long wooden shield. He carried no other weapon but a small, stone hunting knife.

As the Ban'thorn he was riding turned sideways, birdlike, to get a better view of the situation, Gurund Ritroon saw Mnir'ra, who rode behind the little red man. Her complexion was light rose, or sea-shell pink. Her voluminous hair was a glistening soft blue that combined the shades of sea and sky. Her eyes, which looked directly into his with a childlike, searching intentness, were pools of midnight. She wore sandals and filmy trousers, laced tight at the ankles and full to the hipline, where they seemed to become part of her body, terminating at the waist. She wore nothing else except a black cloak over her shoulders, which was held there by two straps that met between her collar bones under a beautiful, jewel-studded medallion, the symbol of her royal rank. It was a glistening, twelve-pointed star, resting between two pale rose breasts which seemed to the god-man who looked at her to be the crowning jewels of her adornment.

Time went on, but nothing happened. He only stared at the little blue-haired queen, caught as though in a magic spell by her eyes. And she, herself, appeared to be in some sort of spell, for her companion noticed her attitude with some wonderment.

"Y'uj'ijo e'si'ia uz'o?" he called, and the god-man understood: "Who are you?" Djik'ri had asked. "And where do you come from?"

In their own language, he shouted back in a mighty voice that crashed boomingly above the waterfall: "You know who I am and whence I come, else you would not have ridden here to find me!"

He saw Mnir'ra's eyes widen with wonder and delight, and she cried out to her brother in a silvery voice, but her words were lost in the roar of the waterfall. Djik'ri guided his mount unhesitatingly into the pool and it swam, though somewhat unwillingly, in his direction. It did not like his large proportions and it let out cackling cries of alarm to express the opinion. But Djik'ri goaded it on, relentlessly, like the master rider he was.

The god-man held his ground, waiting for them. He smiled reassuringly as they approached. When they came up on the shore about six yards from where he squatted, they dismounted. The Ban'thorn immediately ran to the seashore and waited there at a safe distance.

THE TWO beautiful little people stood where they were, hesitant, just slightly fearful of him. For to them he was of heroic proportions, white of skin—which was alien—so white, in fact, that he seemed to glisten like shining marble. He was even taller than the dreaded Bi'djar Ri, taller, perhaps, than even Gon'ri the Warrior. If they could see him standing up they knew he would be fully as tall as a god should be, a tall, shining god, as was Gur, in ages past.

Then he did stand up, and he began to walk toward them, but that seemed to be a mistake, because they both retreated, instinctively, in spite of their great hope that he was the one they sought. So then he stood still.

"I am Gurund Ritroon," he said. "I come from the Outer Emptiness, which lies beyond the Lens."

At once, the other two dropped to their knees and bowed their heads, with arms and fingers extended in his direction.

"Hail, Son of Gur, the Avenger!" he heard Mnir'ra cry out. "Thanks be to Gur that you did not fail us in our time of need! The ancient promise is fulfilled!"

The god-man hesitated. He knew precisely the role he was to play, knew he had great strength, perhaps even immunity from physical harm. But not all was clear to him. He did not know what powers he possessed, if any. He was vaguely disconcerted that his plan and strategy were not clear and certain in his mind, that he should be compelled, like any man, to think of each step he must take as each circumstance presented itself. What was a god supposed to do?

"Arise," he said, for want of anything more appropriate to say.

Whereupon the red man arose, as did his female companion. He took her hand and led her slowly toward the god-man, close, enchantingly close. The god-man's deep blue eyes looked down into hers, and she colored deeply in her embarrassment.

"You are Mnir'ra Nikin'ra, Queen of the Serin Ni," he told her. "I have heard your prayer, and I am here."

Without knowing why, he reached out his hand, as that dimly remembered other self might have done. Djik'ri was the first one to take it. Instead of merely shaking it, however, he fell to one knee and pressed it humbly to his forehead. His own hand was surprisingly firm and strong. Gurund Ritroon looked upon Djik'ri and found that he was worthy.

Then came the thrilling thing he had been waiting for. Mnir'ra, she of the dream-clouds of sky-blue hair, reached out and gently took his hand. When he felt that doll-like hand in his and saw her glowing smile and her moist, welcoming eyes, he felt some of the strength go out of his legs momentarily, and he was breathless.

"You are exceedingly fair," he said, as she kneeled and touched his hand to her forehead.

Then her dark eyes looked up again into his. She said nothing, but she smiled as she had before and his head swam...

After a while, he began to be aware of what Djik'ri was saying to him:

"And of course we will rebuild the ancient temple. But first of all, I hope that it is your wish to aid us in our cause against the Bi'djar Ri, for this is the Season of Urg. I have pledged my life to resist the increasing pressure which has been brought to bear on us, and if you would lead my army against the superior forces of Gon'ri the Warrior, I stand ready to command them for you. But there is little time, if you would put into effect any plans of your own, for even today my sister must begin the task of selecting the victims of the sacrifice."

GURUND RITROON looked into Mnir'ra's eyes and saw tears. They were tears of sorrow, tears of dread, and tears of supplication. He looked for a long while in wondering silence at the two beautiful red people before him. And he struggled desperately to find within himself the power to help them. Again came the unanswered question: What must a god do?

Then he remembered his other self, the Earthman, Flannigan. Flannigan, who had needed his god-self to reach the Lens. Now, beyond the Lens, the god needed the man, Flannigan. Flannigan, Master of Science. That was it! Superior knowledge! Therein lay his power!

A grim smile crept over the lips of Gurund Ritroon. He was getting ideas from the Outer Emptiness, from Flannigan, man of Earth.

"How many red men and how many green men are there?" he asked.

Djik'ri's brows furrowed as he wondered why a god should ask questions. But he hastened to reply. "Of red men there are many, about fifty thousand," he said. "We do not know the number of the Bi'djar Ri, since we have never been to their country—that is, and returned."

"How many ships do they have?"

"We do not know, as they bring only enough to carry back the victims of Urg. Although the last time I recall there were several extra ships full of armed warriors, including Gon'ri himself, who looked with too much interest upon our fair shores and wooded hills. Perhaps each time now he will send more ships until there will be a sufficient number to carry out an invasion."

Gurund Ritroon was getting an inspiration. His grim smile turned to one of enthusiasm. He looked at Mnir'ra.

"The young men and women whom you are going to select for the tribute of Urg will not have to go if they are willing to work for their own salvation," he said. "As you select them, send them to me. Also, send me as many others as you can, but in strictest secrecy. We have enemies, even in Serin-Gor. Surprise must be one of our weapons, but I will give you others, Djik'ri, you must stay here to help me, as much as you can. There is much you and your people will have to learn and do, and the time is short."

Djik'ri's face lighted with fierce elation. Mnir'ra's eyes again glistened with tears, this time out of joy and gratitude.

She reached out and took his hand once more. She knelt before him and touched his hand to her forehead. Moved by an irresistible impulse, he reached out with his other hand and gently stroked her sky-blue hair, so fine it was even difficult to feel. On a further impulse, he pulled her to her feet and drew her close so that each was aware only of the other's eyes. She was so close that they touched, and her doll's body seemed vibrant, soft and warm. Then, as though it were inevitable, he kissed her on her forehead.

Djik'ri stared at him in openmouthed amazement. Mnir'ra hastily withdrew, her shell-pink coloring deepening to rose-red. She signaled goodbye to her brother and ran shyly toward the distant Ban'thorn. And in less than a minute she was galloping away into the woods, leaving Djik'ri alone with their strange new god.

Gurund Ritroon stood there, wondering if he had been motivated more by the god in him or the Irishman.

Djik'ri heard him mutter a great and powerful incantation. It was a cryptic, magic thing that he knew was not for his ears, and he turned respectfully away, even though the English language was incomprehensible to him.

For Gurund Ritroon waved his arms in the air and said aloud to himself, "What will she be thinking of you now, you blasted idiot! A fine god you're making yourself out to be—kissing leprechauns!"

CHAPTER FOUR
"Spears Shine Forth"

ZRAND'Rl, High Priest of Gur, suspected that something was amiss. The citizens of Serin-Gor were a naive people who could not very well dissimulate. By their very secretiveness he knew that something of momentous proportions was brewing. As nothing of momentous proportions, other than Urg, had ever occurred in his memory, the thing was extraordinarily strange.

The more suspicious he became, the more he found that gave him cause for suspicion. He was aware of secret meetings behind closed doors, of lights burning in various windows until the small hours of the dawn. Services in the Temple of Gur were alarmingly reduced, even though the Season of Urg had always served to increase the attendance previously. Reports filtered in concerning, the movement of large groups of people to the other side of Mag'dur. And where was Djikn Kinri the Hunter, who was soon to claim the throne from the regency of his sister? His absence lent particular significance to the unprecedented occurrences. Finally, when Zrand'ri saw crews of men erecting strange devices on the beaches as though in preparation against an invasion, he took action.

The small army of Serin-Gor existed merely as the result of ancient tradition. Complete lack of battle experience had always been a weakening factor as far as effectiveness was concerned, but at least it consisted of more than three thousand men, and they were reasonably disciplined. In later years, since the death of old King Jith'loor, who had walked alone in Zi'ilgar-Lon to find eternal sleep after the accidental death of his wife, Ank'torna, the Counselors of the Queen Regent had organized the management of the army temporarily under the priesthood of Gur, largely owing to Zrand'ri's own eloquent arguments, and thus the High Priest enjoyed the commanding generalship, a privilege which would end upon Djik'ri's maturity and his consequent acquisition to the throne. In the meantime, Djik'ri was a high officer in command of several regiments. But the army knew that Zrand'ri, for the time being, was the commanding general.

For this reason Zrand'ri called in one of his most trusted generals and said, "What is the meaning of building defenses without my orders? And where is Djikn Kinri?"

The man on the carpet was of a heavy, red complexion, a cruder type than most of the Serin Ni. He was Zrand'ri's closest confidant because their temperament was similar, and he had given his entire allegiance to the High Priest for purposes of personal advancement. Also, he despised Djik'ri because he knew that, although their ranks were equal, Djik'ri was the better man, and moreover he was soon to be king and would then take over the army command from Zrand'ri, his benefactor. It was a strong case of professional jealousy, and Zrand'ri knew he would like to see any possible obstacle placed in Djik'ri's path to keep him from becoming king.

"I am pleased to tell you," he said, "that I have been making a thorough investigation of this affair and I have gathered many very startling pieces of information. My report would have been made to you tomorrow, anyway, if you had not called me in. But I'm glad you did, because it's high time for action."

ZRAND'RI looked unimpressed. "You have told me nothing so far," he admonished.

"Very well, I shall make my report. It seems that the Queen and General Djikn Kinri have put out a secret call for volunteers. They are uniting all of Djik'ri's companies and deserters from other units and all of General Djur Djinri's companies under one command and have also enlisted the group chosen for Urg into their work. They are working very secretly, because it appears that they wish to make as much progress with their plans as possible before you take action to oppose them, as they presume you will do in view of your position as High Priest, in charge of the Urg Law jurisdiction."

Zrand'ri's face darkened in rage at knowledge of this maneuver of Djik'ri's. "What is Djik'ri's objective in all this?" he asked, trying to control himself long enough to get the story straight.

The general watched his chief closely as he replied. "Djik'ri, on the Day of Urg, which is also the day when he becomes king, intends to abolish the Law of Urg by resisting the green men."

Zrand'ri's mouth dropped agape. His fierce eyes stared at his informer. "I knew," he said, "that Djik'ri was against the Law of Urg, but I did not know that he would have the courage or knowledge to move so soon. He is a fool! Does he not know that this defiance of Gon'ri the Warrior will precipitate a disastrous invasion upon us?"

"Now we come to the most astounding part of my report," replied the general. "Djik'ri has an ally."

"A *what?*"

"An ally. My agents have gone to the other side of Mag'dur, to the site of the ancient temples, and they have seen him."

"*Him?*" queried Zrand'ri, mystified. "Do you mean that Djik'ri's ally only consists of one man?"

"Yes, but what a man. Perhaps you will appreciate what I mean when I tell you that they call him—Gurund Ritroon!"

Zrand'ri's eyes widened with sudden fear, and he staggered back, one hand raised before him as though to ward off a physical blow.

The name was self-explanatory—Gurund Ritroon, *Son of Gur, the Avenger!*

After a long moment of silence, Zrand'ri's face darkened with suspicion. "I do not believe it!" he said. "What does this imposter look like?"

Again the general watched Zrand'ri as he answered him. He, himself, wanted to know on which side lay the truth, for many strange things were happening. "He is taller than us, taller even than any green man," he said. "He is not of this world, for he is purest white and glistens like polished marble, and his hair is black, and his strength is the strength of a score of Zats. He speaks our language and says that he has come from the Outer Emptiness, from beyond the Lens."

ZRAND'RI was thinking fast. If the physical description were true, then he was truly not of this world. But where could he have come from? Had Gur actually sent the Avenger, after all? Zrand'ri had never really believed the old legend of the Lens.

"No!" he exclaimed in jealous rage. "He cannot be Gurund Ritroon! Gur would have notified me of his coming! If he be an emissary of any god, then he is an enemy in our midst, serving the bloody gods of the Bi'djar Ri in an attempt to undermine us. If he succeeds in deceiving our people, this can be the end of Serin-Gor! I must go and see him at once with my own eyes!"

"I am at your service, Zrand'lir Nzinri," said the general.

"What is this...this false god's plan?" asked Zrand'ri concernedly. "What is he doing?"

"He has them all working," replied the other. "In the mountains they go searching for samples of unusual substances, and they are digging up the ground, taking out many things such as the black stone of fire, which the god-man calls 'co-al'. And there are great, glowing fires where another type of earth is melted down and a liquid substance comes out that, when hardened, becomes black metal. There are huge mill stones turned by many people, and the red, glowing metal is pressed by them into sheets, for shields and armor. They are making strange new weapons. There is one called 'Vee-One' that is a new type of bow with a strange metallic coil in it that can hurl fire brands at the enemy faster and farther than the arrows of the green men. For the first time this puts the Bi'djar Ri in our range before they can get close enough to shoot us, should they attempt to invade us one day."

"I see," said Zrand'ri, fuming. "And what are these contraptions they are erecting on the beaches?"

"They are called 'Vee-Two'," replied the general. "They consist of a series of huge catapults made of entire trees bound cleverly together. These will be used to throw huge rocks out to sea and sink the ships of the green men as they approach. I believe there is a variation of this called 'Vee-Three'. The god-man has sent people to bring back great jars of the black liquid of fire from the bubbling pools beyond Kild'rn, even from the edge of Zi'ilgar-Lon. Flaming cauldrons of this black fire liquid may also be hurled out to sea by means of the catapults to smash into masts and sails of approaching ships and set them afire. Great is the knowledge and cleverness of this stranger."

"Hm-m-m. Very clever. And I suppose he has some other 'Vee' weapons in production?"

"Oh, many others which could not be sufficiently analyzed because of their strangeness and variety, and even those working on the projects did not understand the nature of what they were preparing. Some there are who cook and ferment plant and earth substances to produce searing acids which, when put to work in some strange way with the soft, heavy metal, *gus'drun,* and the black stone, *d'ril,* produce a mysterious, invisible form of life that can bite without leaving a mark on you. And there is a black powder they have made which, when ignited, explodes with a blinding light and can tear down walls of stone. My men have even seen a strange thing that sears the sky with a streak of flame at night and lands afar in the forests, blasting trees and rocks asunder, like a thunderbolt of the gods. It is a powerful magic this god-man is giving them, but secrecy there is very great, and all but one of my spies were apprehended and killed. There is very high morale among Djik'ri's men, and he has several thousand civilians working for him also. Beyond Mag'dur the seashores and the hills and forests are loud with the sounds of unceasing labor, day and night. They have even rebuilt one of the ancient temples for this man-god to live in, and they have clothed him in the raiment of a great king, and they worship at his feet. It is truly a great deception of the people, as you say."

Zrand'ri's dark brows lowered in his frustration. He glared for a long while into space. Then, suddenly, he gave a command.

"Call in every army officer'," he said, "who is loyal to Gur and who has the future safety and welfare of Serin-Gor at heart! This false god who has come among us has bewitched Djikn Kinri into believing that he is doing good for his country, when in reality he is playing right into the hands of the Bi'djar Ri, giving them a legitimate chance to invade us! What are these few new weapons against the unnumbered hordes of green men under Gon'ri the Warrior, whose armor is also of metal and whose ships can fill Ces'son Nar to the horizon, and whose heart is merciless for all the Serin Ni? There is no time to lose if we would save our country! Call the army to me! Tell them that I, Zrand'ri, proclaim this white giant to be an imposter! He comes not from Gur, but from the blood-hungry gods to whom our innocent youths are sacrificed! And he hungers only after more! He is after our destruction! If they love their country and if they care for Djik'ri or their queen, they will rescue them from their great delusion and oppose this stranger. Tell them that if they would see with a clear eye in this terrible moment of bewitchment they should cling to me, Zrand'ri, for I am not deceived! Go!"

EVEN TO A man more shrewd than the general, Zrand'ri would have been impressive, making this impassioned speech. The general left, half stumbling over himself to get out of the temple.

While Zrand'ri waited for the army chiefs to come to him, he climbed into the temple tower where he kept a strange pet. This was a huge black *Ich'nu,* not indigenous to

Serin-Gor, a secret gift given to him by none other than Gon'ri the Warrior in recognition of his Quisling allegiance. The *Ich'nu* was a species of homing bird with a serpent's head and deadly fangs, of great wingspread and an untiring strength. Gon'ri was taking no chances. He had been informed about Djikn Kinri's coming kingship and all about his strong temperament and resentment of the Law of Urg. Should anything unusual develop, the agreement was that he was to be warned ahead of time by means of the *Ich'nu.*

The upper priesthood of both continents knew a sort of cunieform symbolism which was akin to writing, by means of which they could transmit secret messages. Zrand'ri prepared such a message on the silky bark of the *kimblor* tree and rolled it up so that it would fit into a small wooden cylinder attached to the leg of the *Ich'nu.* Once he had it well fastened in and secured, he released the great bird. It spread its somber wings and glided silently away over the Barrier Sea without the slightest hesitation. Zrand'ri watched it go, thinking of the cryptic message he had prepared:

Spears shine forth;
Dark clouds appear;
The fortress is tall and thick…

What this meant was that treachery was in the air and that Serin-Gor was preparing new weapons and was getting ready to resist. It also said that the resistance would be very strong, which meant that the Bi'djar Ri should come full armed for battle.

Thus did Zrand'ri try to earn his chance at the Quisling kingship of Serin-Gor, in case Gon'ri the Warrior's plan of conquest should be carried out.

Much smaller things than political intrigue oft times affect the course of history, however. One such small thing was Zrand'ri's belfry boy. He had been assigned the duty of feeding the *Ich'nu*, and he had learned whence it had come. When Zrand'ri released the weird creature, he made sure the boy was not present, but there was nothing to prevent the boy from seeing it from the hills of Rurz'tlid as it winged its way across the Barrier Sea. And much he wondered about Zrand'ri's purpose in releasing it...

GON'SR LIT'RI, known to fame as Gon'ri the Warrior, was physically, politically and financially the most powerful green man on all the planet of Gra'ghr, which was not an inconsiderable achievement inasmuch as the land of Bi'djar-Tan consisted of a great continent teeming with hundreds of thousands of restless green men, all of them warlike, often fighting wars of their own against each other, galloping thousands strong across the deserts and mountains astride their fighting Ban'thorns, causing lesser kingdoms and principalities to rise and fall like the restless tides of Ces'son Nar. Many were the powerful chieftains who would have risen against Gon'ri had he not learned to rule them all with a hand more ruthless and merciless than their own.

In his sandals, he stood all of two feet in height. A love of rough sports and bloody experience in battle had given him a very powerful and impressive looking body. Like all of the Bi'djar Ri, he was as hairless as the carnivorous *karnger* cat that sat chained beside his throne, and a slight tendency to exude oily moisture from his skin kept his body glistening.

His habitual apparel consisted of a split skirt, open on each side, from the belt line down the thighs. The skirt was heavy with gold braid and weird, jeweled designs connected with his polytheistic religion. The belt he wore was a pure band of gold which supported, besides the skirt, a very long, jeweled fighting dagger. On each powerful forearm he wore two bright bands of silver. They were kept in place by the size of his muscles and were there to remind him, should they ever slip, that he must keep his strength up to par.

A single scar located symmetrically between his brows added dramatic effect to his perpetual frown, Gon'ri had never been seen to smile or heard to laugh in his life. And small wonder. He had witnessed every live sacrifice in the capital since he was old enough to understand, which was thousands of years ago. But he was a great supporter of the sacrifices. Criminals were usually sacrificed, and the word "criminal" was taken to mean any and all enemies. Therefore the threat of the sacrifice gave him power. It gave the priesthood power, and the priesthood was his machine of state. It was a tradition, a way of life which was a part of the social structure of green-man civilization. The worship of their terrible stone gods and the live sacrifices were vital.

But with the growth of the population, which could not be curbed even by recourse to wars or sacrifices, there was a greater incidence of those who got ideas about overthrowing the system, not because they were loath to sacrifice whom they pleased, but because they, too, were hungry for power. So Gon'ri felt that he not only needed a greater source of victims for the sacrifice than that provided by the Law of Urg; he knew that it would be healthy also to satisfy the appetites of his stronger chieftains by initiating a campaign of conquest against the Serin Ni.

AS HE STOOD that evening at a window of his palace in the green-man city of Inis'dur, he gazed reflectively at the leaden, windy sky, the bleak stone buildings, and at the gray granite cliff walls of the stony mountains beyond the city. He missed the sunny skies of Serin-Gor, and its green wooded hills and sparkling streams and flowered plains, and he longed for the arrival of the time to make the journey to pick up the sacrifice victims on the Day of Urg. Just as he ached with inaction, so did the whole nation. Somehow the action must be provided. His desires fought with superstition in his dark soul. Would Gur fall upon him, after all, for breaking the old commandment? Or was the story of the Lens but the fiction of the red men, to save their skins? He had always scorned the ancient legend outwardly, and in his heart he had tried to.

At that moment, a priest entered the room and came to his side, excitedly. He, too, was a bald, oil-exuding green man, but of much smaller stature and of a much more slender build. On his forehead dangled the emerald symbol of his priestly station, meaning that he was one of the dreaded Sacrificers.

"Gon'ri!" he exclaimed, holding out to him a curious scroll of tree bark. "This is amazing news!"

The ruler of the Bi'djar Ri, without change of expression, turned and took the bark. He unrolled it and looked at the cryptic ideograms drawn there. "What does it say?" he asked. "Where did you get it?"

The wiry priest could hardly contain his elation. "Your last question should be answered first," he said. "It comes from our good friend Zrand'ri of Serin-Gor, brought by the *Ich'nu* you gave him!"

Gon'ri tensed, outwardly subduing his excitement. He grasped the priest's arm in a painful grip, while he gave him back the bark scroll. "Read this!" he commanded.

The priest paraphrased the symbols expertly. "Zrand'ri wishes to advice that the people of Serin-Gor are gathering together to resist us on the next Day of Urg. There is much secret activity and preparation of new and powerful weapons. He further states that in his own opinion we should be careful because the resistance is going to be strong."

"Ha!" cried Gon'ri, showing his white teeth without smiling in his high elation. "The red men are taking the first step to break the ancient pact! We offered them peace and freedom in return for obedience to the Law of Urg. Now if they resist us they free our hands! We may attack at will!"

"You are right!" replied the priest. "This is evidence enough, because it comes on the personal authority of Gur's own High Priest. It is an official declaration that the treaty of Urg is being broken. Therefore, it is your solemn duty to invade!"

GON'RI WAS moved to smile, but instead he staggered with the effort of self-composure. He went over to a stone bench and sat down to get a grip on himself. Still he did not smile, and his scarred frown only deepened.

"I hope," he said, "that those songbirds will be able to put up enough resistance to make it interesting for us. The war chieftains of Bi'djar-Tan are restless and filled with a fierce appetite for physical activity. This must satisfy them. Call in my Counselors of War!" he ordered. "I want to assemble our local naval forces and the regular army for a surprise attack, well before they expect us!"

When the excited priest hurried out of the chamber, Gon'ri got up and walked meditatively under a low arch that gave access to his throne room, and for the first time there was the slightest suggestion of a cold smile about his lips.

On the low dais, beside the throne, sat Wur'lun, his great, hairless *karn-ger* cat. He yawned, showing three rows of shark-like teeth in his cavernous, toad-shaped mouth, and his three ruby-red eyes blinked at his master sleepily. The largest, most powerful and deadly carnivore on the planet, capable even of handling several Zats at a time, he was the king of beasts, and apparently he considered it quite appropriate to lie on the throne dais of Gra'ghr's green-man emperor.

Gon'ri walked over to a large stone table that stood below the throne. On it rested a fresh cageful of *lur'lurs*, furry white, rabbit-like creatures that squealed in terror every time that Wur'lun moved.

Gon'ri stared at the *karn-ger* cat. "What do you think, Wur'lun?" he said. "The red-skinned minstrels think they can fight! So that means we move upon them!" The scar between his brows grew dark with shadow and the suggestion of a smile on his lips stiffened into a contemptuous sneer. "And Zrand'ri would be my puppet king of Serin-Gor! Pah!" He opened the cage and extracted a squealing *lur'lur*. He held it in his arm and stroked it reassuringly until it calmed down. "I'll be emperor of Gra'ghr," he said to Wur'lun, who watched the *lur'lur* intently. "And I'll rule from sunny Rurz'tlid by the

River Toor, where Mnir'ra the Singer will sing—and swim—for my personal entertainment."

Wur'lun filled the throne room with a reverberating growl, and Gon'ri raised an eyebrow at him. "What of Djikn Kinri the Hunter?" he asked. In the same instant he cracked the spine of the *lur'lur* so that it was crippled, and he tossed it to his pet. "A good question, Wur'lun—and there is your answer!"

At last, Gon'ri the Warrior smiled, as he watched the *karn-ger* cat eagerly devour the broken and bleeding animal. But it was a cold smile of lofty amusement...

CHAPTER FIVE
The Irish in Him

GURUND RITROON had to admire the red men. They had not even discovered, as yet, the principle of the wheel, yet they took remarkably to his production methods and proved to be really constructive.

The whole shoreline for the distance of a mile from his rebuilt temple was an open-air factory and armed camp. He had the Serin Ni divided into specific work groups and progressive training units, under Djik'ri's able generalship and that of his friend, Djur Djinri. Even little Mnir'ra had settled here for a while. Gurund Ritroon's encouraging plan had inspired her to finish her previously odious task of selecting the victims of Urg. They were all selected in record time and were there on the beach breaking production records, for they worked for their own salvation.

Group One had graduated back to Rurz'tlid, where they were building Vee Twos, the catapults for coastal defense. This project was already in the finishing stages and the coast artillery units of the army had already been selected and trained to man these weapons.

Group Two was still busy advancing the project on Vee One-crossbows. He, himself, tempered the metal and turned out the springs and the red men manufactured the wooden parts and the metal-tipped arrows and the oil-dipped fire brands. Over five hundred Vee Ones were already in the hands of Djik'ri's infantry.

Group Three was working on chest armor and metal shields, and most of the bowmen were already equipped. He kept Djur Djinri busy training infantry in defense and commando tactics, using crossbows, spears, spiked bludgeons, in closed and open fighting, and even in judo.

Strategic Group Four was split into two sections. One did his coal and iron mining and brought him natural oil and sulphur and saltpeter and made charcoal, while the other section made use of the ingredients thus supplied.

Group Five was under strict secrecy.

They were putting together his major Vee-weapons under his personal supervision, but he doubted that he could get these latter ready in time to be effective for the first attack by Gon'ri the Warrior. They all knew now, thanks to Zrand'ri's belfry boy, that the green men had probably been tipped off ahead of time, and that the battle might begin well before the Day of Urg. The least Gurund Ritroon hoped for was that the green men's first assault would be driven back, and that Gon'ri's subsequent preparations for a major invasion would then give him a chance to set up his major weapons. These latter were complicated, and he was handicapped for want of time and suitable materials, but at least he had gunpowder, a small supply of crude copper wire, and wet cell batteries, a few makeshift vibrators and spark coils. He doubted that he could do all he hoped to do, but he was determined to try—and he was teaching Djik'ri as fast as the bewildered little red warrior could take it...

"WE CANNOT express our gratitude to you," Djik'ri told him one night before the Day of Urg. "You are changing the destiny of a planet."

Gurund Ritroon was standing over a crude anvil, sweating over the task, fashioning two halves of a hollow iron ball. This was Vee Ten, the nature of which Djik'ri understood, thanks to his teaching.

"We cannot allow ourselves to be overconfident," he cautioned, tossing a mop of dark hair off his forehead. "Your army is divided. Zrand'ri seems to be producing some effective counter-propaganda, and many units have remained under his command. Having a split army at this time is not good."

Djik'ri smiled confidently. "With our superior weapons we could repel the Bi'djar Ri with half our number."

"Let us not be too sure of ourselves," retorted Gurund Ritroon. "Treachery behind your back while you are fighting for your life is a deadly handicap, often a fatal one. You must make every effort to unify the armed forces of Serin-Gor."

"But Zrand'ri has convinced many of them that you are an emissary of the enemy gods, and that you seek to deceive us," replied Djik'ri. "He, too, can appeal to the men on the basis of patriotism and loyalty, as well as the fear of breaking the Law of Urg. What we are doing, you know, serves to justify a green-man invasion, according to the terms of the ancient pact."

"Djik'ri," said Gurund Ritroon. "Are you, too, torn by doubts? Are you unsure of yourself?" Then he regretted that he had said this, for when he looked at Djik'ri he saw such an expression of hurt pride as he had never witnessed before, in this land or in the world of the Earthman, Flannigan.

Djik'ri became rigid. He turned without a word and stomped out of the workshop.

"Wait!" said Gurund Ritroon, dropping his work.

He overtook Djik'ri on the broken steps of one of the temple ruins. Several hard-working red men had paused to witness the scene. Their young king-to-be stood stiffly and coldly determined, one hand on the handle of his knife. His black eyes blazed into Gurund Ritroon's.

"I can't have even you accuse me of indecision or cowardice!" he said. "I want you to know that even without your help I should have defied the Bi'djar Ri!" With this he turned on his heel and walked away.

Gurund Ritroon was so chagrined over this incident that he could do no more work that night. He was as fond of Djik'ri as he might have been of his own brother. In fact, he was proud of him. But now he had offended him and he felt, in his god-loneliness, that he had lost a much-needed friend.

He walked down to a secluded spot on the beach, away from the large red-man camp and their fires. He sat down on the still warm sand and looked out to sea. Flannigan, the human shadow within him, was in control of his emotions this night, and he allowed the human alchemy of desire to undermine an otherwise cosmic perspective. Gurund Ritroon was humanly lonely now, which was quite different from god-loneliness.

LAN BA'NA was moving swiftly, almost perceptibly, toward the horizon of Ces'son Nar, casting a peculiarly golden moon path on the waters. And Ral, the purple moon, lagged behind, farther up in the sky. The whole scene provided an unearthly beauty which stirred embers of memory in the man Flannigan which had been all but forgotten by his race. This was true enchantment. He did not have to imagine he was in wonderland. He was.

As the camp settled down for the night, sounds diminished to the point where the soft singing of the bards predominated in the cool, moonlit night. As an Earthman, he had heard that saddest of all musical instruments, the Quichuan *quena* of the Peruvian Andes, but this singing of the bards of Serin-Gor outclassed the *quena*. Sometimes the intricately harmonized notes quivered through him like an invisible current, shaping his mind and heart irresistibly to their mood.

Then he was suddenly startled to hear, somewhere close to him, the fairy singing of a red woman:

> *Whither has my lost love gone?*
> *Altinra, she of laughter,*
> *She whose eyes were like the dawn*
> *Where night embraces day...*

He tensed, uncontrollably. This was the old song, the song that had connected him to his strange destiny. At last, here was the Singer, the one who knew the other verse! With an awareness of destiny being fulfilled, he listened for the rest of it, the other part that he had never been able to quite recall before...

> *She who sings no more of me,*
> *Who walks into Eternity,*
> *Taking only memory*
> *Of love, like blossoms, withered.*

> *Why, my love, is fate so cold,*
> *To fill the heart in vain,*
> *Giving today to have and hold,*
> *Only to lose again?*

Meaning dies and beauty's left
Alone in desert's waste.
O leave me not of thee bereft!
I follow thee in haste!

Gurund Ritroon got to his feet. He looked into the darkness in the direction of the singing, and he became aware of an approaching figure. It was a woman, one of the perfectly formed little red women. He thought he knew who it was, but he knew certainly that whoever it was he had waited to find her throughout an eternity.

And then his heart gave a great leap, because it was the one he had hoped it would be—Mnir'ra, distant daughter of Altinra!

She came wearing white flowers in her hair. Her perfect little feet, like those of a miniature pink porcelain gazelle, were bare. She wore only a cool, split skirt, open down the thighs. Traditionally, she wore nothing above her waist but her own beauty. To both his god senses and his human senses she was a treat to the tranquility of his soul. He was not only irretrievably cast away into an alien sphere of existence; he was impossibly in love with a leprechaun!

"Gurund Ritroon!" she called to him, in a happy tone of voice. "How wonderful it is to find you alone!"

"You took the words out of my mouth," he translated the Earthman's emotions into Gra'ghorian speech. "What are you doing here?"

"I came hoping to find you," she said. She had reached his side now and she placed one small hand on his arm as she looked up with a glowing smile into his face.

TO ALL her intoxicating, elfin beauty she had added the scent of an exotic perfume—some sort of flower oil with which she had bathed her entire body so that it glistened softly in the moonlight.

Gurund Ritroon's head swam. Every ounce of manhood in him urged him to take her up in his arms and tell her she had to belong to him. But something troubled the god in him. It was the memory of another love, Altinra, who walked alone in Zi'lgar-lon, the Desert of Death. Was this the price she had paid for loving a god? And then he knew why. As a god, he had a mission to fulfill. After a while, the Lens would take him back again into the Outer Emptiness, and Mnir'ra, if she loved him, would also walk alone where Altinra had gone in ages past. If he had been only a man, perhaps, yes, but the Son of Gur had a mission to fulfill. To think of himself now would be to destroy the object of his love. He could not permit this to happen.

"Gurund Ritroon," she said softly.

"Yes?"

"Please take me in your arms and hold me."

This request hit him like a thunderbolt. He looked at her with widened eyes. "Hold you?" he gasped. "Why?"

"Because I love you."

His brain whirled. Impossible world; impossible love. But here it was.

He made a herculean effort to control himself, but desire suddenly flattened his inhibitions like a tidal wave crashing through a village of paper dolls, and he swept her into his arms. If her doll-like body had been warm and vibrant before, right now it was a maddening flame!

He kissed her on her lips, while her arms went around his neck, and where their hearts had glowed before, now they melted.

"How can I help myself?" he muttered aloud in English. Then he said to her, "We have to figure this thing out before it is too late. How can we two love each other?"

She only smiled in dreamy happiness as she passed a warm hand over the great square of his chest. "Isn't it already too late to question how or why?" she answered.

"Yes. I mean—but I am not of your world."

Mnir'ra looked at him suddenly with deep understanding. "I know, my dearest," she said. "You are Gurund Ritroon, a god. You are not human." She thought for a moment that the god trembled with resentment at that remark, but it was not the god. It was the Irishman. "Still," she continued, "I remember Altinra, and it seems that I was born waiting for you. I could never love another, and it is better, therefore, that I should love you while you are here and then lose you forever, than never love you at all, I can only love you, beloved. I want to belong, and to be loved, even if you are a god, I know your love has waited for me whole ages in the Outer Emptiness, and so that is why I entrust my love to you."

He set her on the ground. "Let me take you back to camp," he said, almost tonelessly. "I love you, yes. How could I ever deny it? But beyond our happiness lies great pain and I'm asking you if it's worth it? You must sleep on this problem, Mnir'ra."

But Mnir'ra stamped her foot on the ground in sudden anger. "I'll have you know that not even Gurund Ritroon, if that's who you really are, can deny the love offer of Mnir'ra Nikin'ra! I have offered myself to you to own and love as a wife, but now I will see you come crawling to me before I will even think of it again!"

"But Mnir'ra, I—"

"Good night!" she cried bitterly. And she ran away like a little wild animal, her incredible hair floating behind her.

Gurund Ritroon stood still and held both his temples. "Ye gods!" he exclaimed in English. "Two-time loser in one night! Now they're both mad!"

Ruefully, and with many conflicting emotions raging within him, he turned back toward his temple dwelling, where Djik'ri also slept, with the intention of going to bed. However, had he been aware of a thousand or so pairs of hostile eyes peering at him from the woods over the dead bodies of a score of sentinels, he might have slept that night even less than he did.

CHAPTER SIX
Civil War

THE RED men slept peacefully within sight of the new Temple of Gur, which was the symbol of their new-found hope. But there were other red men, in the bordering forest, who regarded the temple as a threat to their very existence, for Zrand'ri's appeal to superstition had turned more than half the army to his side.

Zrand'ri himself was present at the head of this silent army, mounted on a Ban'thorn, surveying the camp in company with the dark redskin who had first reported to him concerning these strange activities.

So far, his plan was working satisfactorily. The major portion of the army was his, he had sent his message in time to Gon'sr Lit'ri, and if he were any judge of the green warrior, he knew that there would soon be warships riding the Barrier Sea. And here, to complete his luck, was a sleeping camp, sentinels all taken care of, and the god-man where he wanted him—inside the temple along with Djikn Kinri, who slept there also, according to Zrand'ri's spies.

"The Queen," he whispered to his general. "She sleeps within the camp this night?"

"I am informed," said the general, "that for some reason unknown to us she started back toward Rurz'tlid to-night with a company of guards."

"You are...ah...taking care of that situation?"

"Yes, your Holiness."

Zrand'ri grinned in triumph. "Good!" he said. "Then proceed at once with orders one and two!"

The general saluted. He signaled to a nearby aide, and the latter raised a long, slender tube to his lips and produced a thin, high, piping sound. As this faint sound reached the ears of the army surrounding him, about one thousand shielded spearmen moved resolutely out upon the beach toward their sleeping countrymen.

Then the general's aide piped again, this time twice in succession. At this signal, a special task force of men heavily laden with special equipment moved in frantic haste toward the newly constructed temple.

DJUR DJINRI was a very conscientious general, a man capable of taking care of his responsibilities. It is owing to such chance virtues as this in times of epic emergency among all civilizations that great national tragedies have been circumvented with only seconds to spare. A hundred generations of red men on the planet Gra'ghr were to revere the memory of Djur Djinri because, besides being a good general, he was a light sleeper as well.

He had heard the gurgling, muffled cry of the last sentinel as he had died at the hands of Zrand'ri's men. Wisely, he did not leap to his feet and cry an alarm, as he knew well the size of the total army, and his own small force of eight hundred men told him that Zrand'ri had about twenty-two hundred at his disposal. Some would naturally be in Rurz'tlid, but there could well be fifteen hundred here, if his suspicions were verified that a major attack was about to start.

Suddenly, campfire light reflected from a score of spears in the woods, and he knew beyond all shadow of a doubt that the worst had come. By mortal struggle, the men of

Serin-Gor were about to weaken themselves in the face of imminent warfare with the Bi'djar Ri.

He weighed the possibilities and consequences swiftly in his mind. If Zrand'ri won, there would possibly even be no Gurund Ritroon to help them against the green men, and no Vee-weapons. This preparation for resistance which had already been made evident would, he knew, precipitate the dreaded green-man invasion upon Serin-Gor and find them unprepared. A small boy who worked in the temple had brought a message to Djik'ri that, seven days ago, Zrand'ri had communicated with Gon'ri the Warrior by means of a *Ich'nu*. This would bring the green-man hordes upon them at any hour. The red men, if caught with divided forces now, would lose, to become slaves to the green men forever!

Like a flash of divine inspiration the thought came to Djur Djinri that here, in this hour, the destiny of a world might be decided, Gurund Ritroon was asleep in the temple, as was Djikn Kinri. He had no way of awakening them, and Zrand'ri might trap them there by barricading the door and windows. Plainly then, the work of salvation rested upon his own shoulders!

Quietly, the general pulled on his armor and checked up on his new crossbow and metal-tipped arrows. At the same time he nudged his neighbor, a blissfully slumbering captain.

"Pass the word along," he said. "But whisper it. Let not a man speak aloud under penalty of death. We are about to be attacked. Get armor and crossbows ready and prepare to execute maneuver three."

By the time Zrand'ri's men stepped onto the beach, many hundreds of Djur Djinri's men were ready and others were getting ready, as quietly and unobtrusively as possible.

"The camp's awake!" cried one invader inadvisably. For his trouble he received a spear in his back, and he was through with speaking forever.

"Attack!" cried Zrand'ri's general, and the invaders hurled their spears at a wall of armored men rising up from the sands.

THE SPEARS bounced off of metal shields and chest armor, while strange, powerful bows shot metal-tipped arrows at them with lightning speed. It was that first counterblow which saved everything, because it withered the invader's ranks enough to equalize the numbers on each side.

From there on it was hand to hand and spear to spear. And many of Djur Djinri's men were still taken by surprise, not having had ample time to prepare themselves. But in the confusion the major portion of armored men were able to escape into the forest, leaving an almost empty camp to Zrand'ri. He could only boast of less than two hundred enemy dead, wounded and captured.

The men under Djur Djinri became Gra'ghr's first guerrilla fighters. With firm purpose, Djur Djinri gathered them together in strategic groups and dispersed them again with a definite plan of action.

"We must remain free," he told them, "to man the coast defenses when Gon'ri comes. Our forces are small, and we may not be led by Gurund Ritroon or Djik'ri, because I believe they were trapped inside the temple, but with what Gurund Ritroon has given us we may be able to turn Gon'ri back for more reinforcements. By the time he returns, Gurund Ritroon may be free. In the meantime, we must also keep Mnir'sr Nikin'ra in mind. Zrand'ri may wish to capture her and take the throne. Therefore, follow these orders. One: Do not form larger groups than a platoon until you hear the password, which is—Urg! When that comes, all converge immediately on the beach defenses at Rurz'tlid and defend your country to the death. Two: In the meantime, stay hidden and well dispersed in the hills surrounding Rurz'tlid. Three: Try to capture officers and men out of the opposition forces under Zrand'ri and convince them that they must join us. Explain our side of the question by saying that we have proof that Zrand'ri is a traitor. He has sent a message to Gon'ri by means of a *Ich'nu* which Gon'ri gave him for that purpose. This means we are in imminent danger of attack, and therefore we must all unite! It is only Zrand'ri who wishes to divide us, because he wants the throne. Djik'ri and Mnir'ra have sworn to me that Gurund Ritroon is genuine, for he came in direct response to their prayers to Gur. Tell them not to become traitors, but to protect their queen and country and follow the banner of Freedom which we have set before us."

The guerrillas actually made a banner that night. It was white, emblazoned with a menacing looking cross-bow and metal-tipped arrow. By morning there were several to unfurl in case sails were sighted on the Barrier Sea...

GURUND RITROON was awakened by Djik'ri, in the temple.

"Wake up!" he shouted. In the light of the torch he held in his hand, Gurund Ritroon observed that his previous expression of proud indignation had been supplanted by one of genuine consternation. "The camp has been wiped out!" he exclaimed. "We're trapped! They've barricaded the door and windows! Zrand'ri's men are outside, his own special guard. You've got to get us out of here! Do you know what this means? Gon'ri the Warrior will invade this country at any hour now and the new defenses will not be manned! Many of the new weapons are stored here in the temple. In spite of all your planning we may be wiped out—conquered! And since I know Zrand'ri wants the throne, he has probably taken Mnir'ra!"

Gurund Ritroon took a great, deep breath and got to his feet. "Mnir'ra? Taken by Zrand'ri?" he said in a rumbling voice. His brows came close together, lowering over narrowed blue eyes. The marble whiteness of his face darkened, and knots of stubborn muscle lifted along his jaws. Now he was Son of Gur, the Avenger, and to his godly strength was added the flaming temper of an Irishman.

"Let's get out of here," he said between his clenched teeth.

"But that's just it!" complained Djik'ri. "We can't get out! They've barricaded everything! And outside are about five hundred of Zrand'ri's men just hoping we'll try to come out into the open!"

"I don't give a damn about those little runts!" Gurund Ritroon broke unconsciously into English. "I want to get out of here! That's all I ask!"

He placed his shoulder to the heavy wooden doors of the temple and heaved mightily. Under the terrific pressure, the thick timbers splintered, but beyond were tons of sandbags and boulders, braced by more timbers. Sweat and strain as he might, he found the barricade too heavy to be moved.

"Great Gur!" moaned Djik'ri. "Why should I be imprisoned like this! Please, Gurund Ritroon! If you are Son of Gur, the Avenger, you must get us out of here!"

The god-man sensed Djik'ri's deep anguish and mortification. For a leader like Djik'ri to be caught in a spot like this at a time of national emergency, he knew, was maddening. He was troubled enough by his own sense of urgency.

"The powder!" exclaimed Djik'ri. "We can blast our way out!"

Gurund Ritroon shook his head. "I could, perhaps, but the size of blast it would take for that barricade might kill you."

"Then let's try the windows!"

"Those niches are too narrow for me, but you might be able to get through one of them." Gurund Ritroon jerked loose one of the heavy timbers sticking out of the shattered door of the temple. He used this as a battering ram, through one of the side window niches. Soon he had crashed through the outside timbers of the smaller barricade, and the pale light of dawn filtered in to them. In their field of vision was the vine-grown side of the steep bluff beside which the temple had been built.

"You could get through that," he told Djik'ri, "but you'd probably be captured."

"One of us must get through and make contact with any survivors who might still be on our side. They must be rounded up to man the beach defenses at Rurz'tlid!" Djik'ri prepared to go through the window. "Once I contact those who are loyal to the throne, I know I can win over a lot of the others from Zrand'ri. It has to be done quickly, because even at this minute there may be sails on Ces'son Nar!"

Gurund Ritroon looked appreciatively at the little red warrior. "All right, Djik'ri," he said. "But don't worry about me. I'll take care of myself. And I'll see you soon."

"But if you go through the front, you'll expose yourself to Zrand'ri's crack troops, and many of them are armed with Vee Ones!"

Gurund Ritroon glared at Djik'ri. "Have you forgotten who I am?" he asked, boomingly. "You forget that the outcome of this struggle was written eons ago, I am the Avenger! Now, have faith, and go!"

WITHOUT another word, Djik'ri climbed into the window niche and pulled himself through. Gurund Ritroon watched him closely as he began to scale the bluff outside.

Then, suddenly, he saw Djik'ri stiffen and throw his head back in pain. A metal-tipped arrow, shot from a cross-bow, had neatly pinned him in the back. He bent over backward, struggled to reach the arrow with one free hand, and then fainted, tumbling down out of sight.

Gurund Ritroon watched speechlessly. He looked stonily through the window niche at a sharp tree root that protruded from the bluff. It dripped Djik'ri's blood. In the brightening dawn light, each drop seemed to be a priceless ruby.

Outside he heard shouts of triumph from Zrand'ri's guards as they scampered toward the temple to claim Djik'ri's body, Gurund Ritroon's fists clenched. There were many solemn things he swore he would accomplish this day.

In less than five seconds he had a long wooden bench up-ended against the temple door. He sprang on top of it and looked through the window niche there. This was too small even for Djik'ri's body, and it was not barricaded. Through it he could see hundreds of red men running in his direction up the beach, brandishing spears, cross-bows and metal shields. In his hand he held Gra'ghr's first version of the bazooka. Grimly, he thrust it through the niche and fired, point blank, at the oncoming men.

Then he was stayed at the sight of the sudden carnage wrought. Twenty of them died instantly, half ripped apart. Others rolled about in bloody agony. Many turned and ran while others groveled on the sand in abject terror. Never in the history of their world had such a weapon been seen or heard. To them it was a thunderbolt of the gods.

After all, thought Gurund Ritroon, these were Mnir'ra's and Djik'ri's people, even if they were revolutionists. He'd have to control his temper and spare them as much as he could, even if the little devils had killed the best man they had—their own kind who might have been their greatest—

"Djik'ri!" he moaned, fighting back the moisture in his eyes. "You poor, brave little leprechaun! They got you in the back!"

After that one bazooka shot, he got busy. There was the matter of blasting his way out of the temple. He loaded the inner side of the barricade behind the splintered door timbers with metal containers of powder and attached a crude but usable home-made fuse. With Djik'ri's torch he ignited it. And then he ran to the far end of the temple, up on the altar, where rested a facsimile of the legendary Lens. He held his ears, hoping that his densified frame could withstand the concussion…

CHAPTER SEVEN
The First Invasion

THAT SAME morning, Djur Djinri's tired guerrillas espied with dismay a great fleet of green-man ships sailing down upon Rurz'tlid. Never had such a force of green men been seen before—fully thirty vessels crammed with warriors. There would be an average of three thousand men on those formidable vessels! And the only body of red men really disposed to resist them numbered six hundred!

Undaunted, General Djur Djinri passed the word along.

"Urg!" "Urg!" "Urg!" sounded the cries of action through the forests above the flowered plain of Raj'dur. Many a bugler lifted the shrill *grin'dnir* gourd to his lips and startled the citizens and the garrison below. From the city, men and women looked up in astonishment to see a small army of six hundred armored men running down upon them, carrying a number of white banners before them. These banners carried the picture of a strange new weapon, that which they brandished in their hands.

Zrand'ri's men quickly organized to resist. There were about a thousand present in the city's garrison. But Djur Djinri's archers, dropping in long lines to their knees to take aim and fire, withered their ranks with crossbow shots long before they came in range of the defenders' ordinary bows. The spearmen rushed for cover in confusion, as did the common citizenry. All were amazed, terrified and bewildered, trying to analyze their precarious predicament and weigh values.

They knew their country was about to be invaded by a dreaded foe, and these brave fighters from the hills seemed to be disposed and equipped to make a defensive stand. Yet Zrand'ri's men opposed the defenders of Serin-Gor!

By the time Djur Djinri's forces gained the city's outskirts, they found Zrand'ri's men and many of the citizens joining their ranks and fighting off the waning opposition.

"Follow the banner of Freedom!" cried the guerrillas. "Zrand'ri the traitor brought Gon'ri upon us! He has captured Mnir'ra and seeks the throne for himself! Down with Zrand'ri! Fight for the Queen and Djikn Kinri—and Gurund Ritroon!"

Zrand'ri, fuming from his temple tower, shot orders at his remaining officers. "Tell them that Gur forbids this sacrilege!" he shouted. "They struggle in vain against a destiny that is written! They must cease all resistance at once!"

But by the time the guerrillas reached the beaches the whole army, with the exception of a few of Zrand'ri's special guards, was with the defenders.

"Down with Zrand'ri!" they shouted. "Long live the Queen! Long live King Djik'ri! Long live Serin-Gor!"

GON'RI THE WARRIOR, from the crow's nest of his flagship, trained his keen eyes upon the distant shoreline and estimated that only about two thousand fighters were there to oppose him.

"I am highly disappointed," he said to his chief adjutant who stood in the crow's nest beside him. "The resistance is less than I thought it would be. However, that is due, no doubt, to Zrand'ri's good work. In a way, I suppose I should consider him for a small reward of some sort."

"I see some fighting around the Temple of Gur," remarked the adjutant. "Zrand'ri must be holding out there."

"It means, no doubt, that he is holding Queen Mnir'ra there. He promised me the Queen in exchange for the throne of Serin-Gor. Make the temple objective number one instead of the palace. Now, you'd better get back on the bridge because we'll soon have them in range of our bows. We want to give them our best volleys before we get within range of their weaker fire."

The adjutant suddenly grasped Gon'ri's arm and pointed at the sky. "Look!" he exclaimed.

And Gon'ri looked. He saw hundreds of long, thin lines tracing their way toward his ships, as though some herculean force had thrown out hawsers to them.

"What is it?" he queried.

"Those are trails of smoke!" cried the adjutant. "Arrows carrying fire! A brilliant weapon, but where did they get it?"

"I find this not so entertaining," frowned Gon'ri. "Signal all ships full sail ahead! We must get on land among those minstrels before they set us all on fire! How do they have a superior range?"

"New type of bow, sire! It looks like you'll get the kind of resistance you wanted! With your permission, I'll go to my station at once!"

The adjutant nimbly slithered down the rigging instead of using the mast ladder. For it was obvious that a serious emergency had arisen. Some of the ships were already throwing up clouds of smoke and flame, their compliments of fighters leaping into the sea.

"Full sail ahead!" shouted Gon'ri from the crow's nest. "All bowmen at stations! Get in range! Full volley! I'll have the head of the bowman who fails to find his mark!"

Filled with excitement and wonderment, keen to the scent of battle in the midst of smoke and flame, the powerful green bowmen crowded the forward gunwales of the full-canvassed ships and held their arrows aimed for the command to fire. Some ships, heavily gutted by flame, were falling behind and wallowing crosswind in the path of others. Suddenly, metal-tipped arrows of death sprang from the shoreline with unforeseen velocity and decimated the ranks of Gon'ri's prize bowmen before they could fire. Scores fell into the sea, clutching at deeply imbedded arrows in hearts and throats and bellies.

"Full speed! Full speed!" shrieked Gon'ri. He had only twenty ships left in the running. Fully ten ships had lost speed because of burning sails. One was capsizing.

BUT JUST as the still formidable fleet brought the red men within range of the green men's bows, a new weapon was brought into play. Not much attention had been given by the enemy to about fifty strange structures lined up along the beaches for about one mile. These looked like tree trunks tied together and bent over by the wind.

Suddenly, these batteries of tree trunks straightened up in many places, and as they did they hurled huge boulders or flaming cauldrons into the sky. Being released at close range over closely riding ships, the percentage of hits was high. The great ponderous rocks came crashing through masts and sails and men, shattering the decks and in some cases going through the hulls. The flaming cauldrons shattered, spewing flame and destruction wherever they hit.

Two ships floundered. Four more were incapacitated with rigging down.

"Faster!" shrieked Gon'ri. "Drive into the shore!"

Then the red men hit the ships with a huge volley of new fire brands. And they again withered the ranks of the green men with crossbow fire. They also released more catapults. Men died on the decks and in the sea. More sails went up in flame. Clouds of boulders and flaming cauldrons descended upon the attackers.

And so it was that, of three thousand battle-hungry green men, only about fifteen hundred succeeded in getting their feet on shore that day. But once on shore, engaged in hand to hand combat, they changed the aspect of the struggle somewhat. For in spite of a sprinkling of armor among the defenders, and in spite of some good archery and spearing and bludgeoning, the green men were larger and stronger, and they pushed their advantage.

Led by Gon'ri himself, one large group pushed rapidly toward the temple to take the Queen…

Djur Djinri's hands were tied with the main defenses of the city, but he was vividly aware of the spearhead that was approaching the temple. Green men and red men dueled with spears and bludgeons. Since metal work on Gra'ghr was still in its infancy, swords were unknown. The spear dueling was a spectacular activity which held a double threat for the weaker contestant. One could go down with a split skull from the hard blow of a spear shaft as well as a pierced abdomen. And it was noisy. Thousands of shafts clattered and banged in the streets of Rurz'tlid, and many a red man as transfixed by a powerfully driven spear. The majority of green men who lay dead had been reached by sniping bowmen from the rooftops.

As best he could, Djur Djinri fought his way toward the temple, forced by the menacing circumstances to leave his station in the hands of lesser officers. Gon'ri's group was close to establishing contact with Zrand'ri's special guards. Fearing that he would not arrive in time to avert the capture of the Queen, Djur Djinri ducked down a side alley, intent upon following a special short cut.

WHEN GON'RI finally did gain the temple, he lost no time in getting down to business. Zrand'ri received him with a triumphant smile, although a worried shadow lingered about his dark eyes. Around his neck was a silver chain which supported a sort of holy water dispenser that dangled against his chest. He was in full regalia for an official visit.

"You have broken the resistance!" he said to Gon'ri. "Hail the ruler of Gra'ghr!"

"Never mind the ceremony, Zrand'ri," barked Gon'ri. "Where is the Queen? We've got to get out of here! Why didn't you tell us about these new weapons? Do you realize we came near to being defeated? Of course I shall return to Bi'djar-Tan to assemble a fleet ten times as large and bring thirty thousand fighters, and I will exterminate every living red man in payment for this day, but you I shall hold especially to blame!"

Zrand'ri's smile quickly faded and his eyes flashed sudden defiance as he backed down the temple aisle toward the Lens—altar of Gur. He fingered the dispenser on his chest nervously. "I have served you well, Gon'ri!" he exclaimed. "Now I want the throne of Serin-Gor in exchange for those services, and in exchange for the Queen!"

Gon'ri's scar sank into the cleft of a frown on his forehead. His muscular spear arm began to rise, the heavy, bloodied point aimed directly at Zrand'ri's chest. But the latter began to laugh.

"Did you think you would find me unprepared against your treachery?" he asked. "You'll never take me, green man!"

And with this he broke the container loose from the chain on his chest, which action also pulled loose a large stopper. In a lightning-swift movement he flung the contents of it over Gon'ri, and the latter dropped his spear to clutch his face in a frenzied effort to claw off his skin. Zrand'ri's men had found one of Gurund Ritroon's storage batteries and had stolen some of the fluid from it. This he had thrown into Gon'ri's face.

In the resultant confusion, he escaped behind the altar through a subterranean passage. But one man, who was climbing into the temple through a back window, saw him and witnessed the trick of the secret exit. It was Djur Djinri. With bloodied spear and battle-scarred shield, he followed Zrand'ri into the secret passage.

He found himself in ancient catacombs that led into a series of natural caverns. The recently ignited oil pots along the walls alerted him to the possibility that Zrand'ri had imprisoned Mnir'ra in this place.

Nor was he long in verifying this suspicion. He passed the open door of a dungeon, and around the next turn in the low-ceilinged passageway he came upon Zrand'ri, who was struggling with Mnir'ra, trying to force her to accompany him. Directly behind them were several openings, one of which appeared to open into the deeper darkness of another cavern.

At sight of him, Zrand'ri struck Mnir'ra, knocking her to the ground and momentarily stunning her before she could cry out. Then he turned with a snarl and dove under Djur Djinri's lunging spear. His wiry arms went around the other's legs and they both crashed to the ground.

In one instant, a foul blow crippled Djur Djinri momentarily, but in the same instant his powerful hands were around Zrand'ri's scrawny neck, and he squeezed to kill. Zrand'ri's clawing fingers tore at his mouth, his nose and his eyes. For a pain-blackened eternity it seemed to be a contest between them to see which could endure this torture the longest.

But Mnir'ra soon recovered sufficiently to pick up Djur Djinri's fallen spear, which she promptly drove into Zrand'ri's back. The High Priest arched backward, breaking the general's grip on his throat, and he screamed, then dropped to the ground.

BEHIND him, Djur Djinri heard the sound of running feet, and he heard shouts in the recognizable accent of the Bi'djar Ri. They had found the secret passage.

"Follow me!" he said to Mnir'ra, leading her into the dark passageway directly ahead of him. He had wrenched his spear out of Zrand'ri's back, but as Mnir'ra took one look behind her she saw the latter crawl painfully into the concealing shadows of a low niche in the corridor's wall.

Unluckily for Djur Djinri, he chose the wrong passage. He soon found himself in a *cul-de-sac,* a small, dark cavern without other opening than that through which they had come. And here the green men came upon him bearing torches and long spears.

Conversation was superfluous. Against absolutely hopeless odds, Djur Djinri fought his way valiantly into

Gra'ghr's hall of eternal fame—and fell sobbing, not from the pain of his mortal wounds, but because of his helplessness to defend his queen…

After a while, he became aware of Zrand'ri standing over him. The High Priest was obviously on his last legs, but he held the business end of a broken spear in both his hands. The wavering light of a torch he had set in the ground accentuated the drawn lines of frustration and rage in his thin face.

"If you had not interfered today," he said. "I should have been ruler of Serin-Gor!"

He tried to raise the spear to drive it down into Djur Djinri's heart, but it required a terrific effort of his will even to stand up, and his movements were slow.

Behind him, Djur Djinri suddenly discerned something that for the first time filled his warrior's heart with dread. Out of a hole in the wall crept a threaded, deeper darkness, an oozing, amorphous thing that spread out across the wall with evil purpose. He knew very well what it was, though few had ever seen one and lived to tell about it. It was a living, almost indestructible web—a deadly Kran'jandoon.

In one supreme effort, Djur Djinri locked the toes of one foot behind Zrand'ri's left ankle, and with his other foot he shoved against the priest's left knee. This maneuver threw the other directly into the clutches of the monstrosity on the wall.

Instantly, Zrand'ri became tangled inextricably in the cloying, powerful web, and he screamed out in his terror, struggling futilely. And Djur Djinri laughed. He laughed because death was not so bitter to him now, because no one could have inflicted upon this traitor to Serin-Gor a most suitable punishment for his crime…

CHAPTER EIGHT
The Avenger

WHEN THE charge went off, the whole temple seemed to leap into the air, and Gurund Ritroon was flattened under a blast of splintered timbers and flying debris. When the smoke cleared, however, he shook his head and got up. There were several dark bruises on him where heavy objects had struck, but otherwise he was unhurt.

He immediately began to prepare himself for battle. Chest armor and a special helmet came first. Then there was a long, heavy, spiked bludgeon that no one else on Gra'ghr could have lifted. On his back was strapped a crossbow and full quiver of metal-tipped arrows, and at his left hip swung a cloth bag filled with crude but effective grenades. Instead of a shield, he carried the bazooka, with extra charges for it in the grenade bag. This weapon was slung over one shoulder, while in his two free hands he carried the mighty bludgeon.

As he stepped over the shattered barricade he was an apparition of terror to the hundreds of men who still waited for him outside. Dead men lay at his feet. Beyond, at a distance of about thirty yards, the rest stood looking at him in awe.

One of the red men, less awestruck than terrified, raised his crossbow in self-defense and fired it, aiming at Gurund Ritroon's neck. The metal-tipped arrow hit its mark, but to the amazement of all, it failed to penetrate the god-man!

The arrow stung painfully, but Gurund Ritroon knew he was fairly safe from all arrows. He reached for his grenade bag, then thought better of it.

"I am Gurund Ritroon!" he bellowed at them. "Zrand'ri is a false priest. Return to Rurz'tlid and defend your country against your true enemies—the Bi'djar Ri!"

Without waiting to see what the effect of his admonition would be, he turned to the bluff side of the temple to look for Djik'ri. He found the spot under the window where the other should have been, but he was not there. In the sand he saw the trail of a man who was bleeding and who had dragged himself painfully along the ground. Gurund Ritroon followed this trail, hopefully.

He did not have far to go before he found him. He lay between two large boulders, unable to crawl farther. Gravely wounded as he was, he looked up at Gurund Ritroon and smiled—then fainted.

Gurund Ritroon picked him up and carried him back to the temple. As he approached the blasted doorway he noticed that the beach had been cleared of Zrand'ri's men. Apparently they had either had a change of heart or decided on a strategic retreat.

In the temple, Gurund Ritroon doctored Djik'ri. He cut the arrow out of his back and cauterized the wound, covering it with a mild poultice and a bandage. Then he strapped his bludgeon to his back and carried Djik'ri in his arms out of the temple and started walking down the beach."

"Where is Mnir'ra?" he asked.

WHEN HE arrived at Rurz'tlid, he marveled at the white beauty of the stone city, in spite of his anxiety concerning Mnir'ra. So preoccupied was he that he failed to notice at first that he met with no resistance. The people who had only heard of him, but never seen him before, hid in their houses and watched him from their secret points of vantage in amazement, and with newly awakening faith in the legend of the Lens. Spearmen who had formerly been under Zrand'ri now huddled on rooftops and watched him warily as he came walking down the middle of the street, carrying the limp form of Djik'ri in his arms. He was taller and stronger even than Gon'ri the Warrior, and he was white as marble. They knew, at last, that this was Gurund Ritroon.

Djur Djinri's guerrillas, under the white banner of the crossbow, gathered in his wake, cheering as they went, but not too exultantly. They seemed worried. In Rurz'tlid and on the beaches were many signs of the recent battle.

Gurund Ritroon knew, on first sight of the place, by the green and red bodies strewn about, that Gon'ri had attacked. And by the wrecked ships not far from shore he knew that the defenders had not done so badly.

But where was Mnir'ra?

Just then, Djik'ri stirred feebly in his arms. Gurund Ritroon saw him looking up at him with a feeble but grateful smile.

"We must find out what happened to Mnir'ra," Gurund Ritroon said to him.

Djik'ri's eyes widened with sudden recollection and alarm. He looked at the spearmen on the rooftops and at Djur Djinri's guerrillas who crowded around him and Gurund Ritroon. He called to one officer nearby.

Gurund Ritroon saw the latter point seaward, and when he looked far out he saw for the first time the upper rigging of several sailing vessels just creeping beyond the horizon.

That was all he wanted to know. He had seen a certain ship in front of him near the shore which was almost intact. It was about twenty-five feet long, with two masts. Dead green men hung over its rails and lay on the deck.

He looked at the ocean waves to measure the wind and saw that it was favorable. So he suddenly laid Djik'ri down among his men and started for the ocean. Amidst cries of alarm and amazement, he waded hip deep into the water and came to the ship.

He placed his weapons and supplies on board and then got back into the water. He placed his hands under the ship's bow and pushed it off the sandy bottom into deep water—a feat which could not have been duplicated on Gra'ghr. Then, pulling himself up a hawser, he clambered on board again, turning his attention to the sails, which he unreefed and set in use. The fair wind filled them, and he began to tack away with the ebbing tide…

"Gurund Ritroon would attack the entire nation of Bi'djar-Tan singlehanded," remarked one of Djik'ri's officers, as he watched the vessel move away. "They may overcome him by trickery or by force, in spite of his marvelous weapons and towering strength. We may never see him again."

Djik'ri had been carried to a rooftop and was being supported by the officer who has spoken. His greenish-blue hair waved about his shoulders as he watched his friend depart. "You do not know him," he replied, "nor are you aware of the inner forces which drive him onward. I believe that his heart is with the Queen."

SEVERAL soldiers surrounding him looked at him with raised brows and opened mouths. "You mean, he is in love?" queried the officer who supported him.

"I am sure of it," said Djik'ri. "He loves Mnir'ra and she loves him. It is the same with them as it was with Gur and Altinra of old." Then he added, "Now tell me what information you have. Where is Zrand'ri?"

"He escaped, sire, through some secret exit in the temple, and Djur Djinri followed him. We know not where these two might be, nor the fate of either."

"Good Djur'ri," said Djik'ri. "His name will not be forgotten by us. I have overheard some of you saying that it was he who led the chief resistance. You must send a detail at once to search the temple for the secret passage. He and Zrand'ri must be found."

"We are already searching, sire."

"Good. Then what of Gon'ri? Did he escape alive?"

"Yes, although we believe he may die. Zrand'ri, upon meeting with deception at his hands, threw over him some of the fiery liquid which Gurund Ritroon made for his boxes of invisible life that bites. Gon'ri's men led him away blind. But the Queen and many of our people went with the Bi'djar-Ri."

Djik'ri's face hardened. "If Gon'ri lives, he will organize another expedition, even in spite of Gurund Ritroon. Our god-friend is driven to vengeance by the emotion of his love, but Gon'ri will be moved to organize the total forces of his people against us, driven by a consuming hatred for us. And who can say which is stronger—love or hate? A god-man or a nation of people? No, we must prepare ourselves quickly to meet an attack ten times the size of the one which you have just suffered. We must go to the temple and take out all of the new weapons and get them ready."

"But, sire, only Gurund Ritroon knows how to work them! Should we not concentrate on the crossbows and catapults alone?"

"You may concentrate on those, yes. Increase your weapons tenfold, twentyfold! Increase the army to its ultimate maximum! Everyone is going to have to fight for his salvation. But give me five hundred men. I remember much of what Gurund Ritroon taught me. Perhaps I could set up what he planned to do himself."

GURUND RITROON sailed all afternoon straight out to sea. He tried to keep his upper rigging just out of sight of the green-man fleet, but he stayed close enough to keep their mast tops visible. Visibility was remarkable due to a crystal clearness of the air not known to Earth except in high altitudes.

As the four suns of Gra'ghr sank below Ces'son Nar and Lan Ba'na appeared, he quickly plotted his course before losing sight of the other ships in the starless darkness, which was relieved only by the lonely, golden moon path on the alien waters. Once he was sure of his direction, he lay down on the deck and watched for the purple moon, Ral, to rise over his starboard bow.

He was thirsty, but he could not find any water on board, although he did find a meager supply of food. On a sudden hunch, he sampled some seawater and found to his surprise that he was sailing on fresh water. Its taste was vaguely bitter, but it was very satisfying to the thirst.

Somewhat relieved by this discovery, he drank freely of the water of Ces'son Nar. It is often upon the ill-advised action of an unguarded moment that unhappy destinies are founded. No one had told him that the waters of the

Barrier Sea were dangerous to drink. They were not harmful to sea life, but if taken internally-deadly poison.

Sometime past midnight, he was in convulsions. After a weakening attack of nausea, he began to have griping pains, accompanied by dizziness. He knew it was due to the seawater, but it was too late to do anything about it. Just as the pain became insupportable he lost consciousness, and the lonely vessel sailed uncertainly toward a distant coastline that was just appearing on the horizon...

CHAPTER NINE
In the Enemy's Camp

WHEN HE regained consciousness, somewhat to his surprise, it was with an awareness of having been out for some considerable period of time. Even before he opened his eyes, he knew that he was unarmed and a prisoner. For he felt many ropes pressing against his bared chest, binding him firmly to the ground.

When he opened his eyes he found that he lay in a great square in the center of a somber-looking city of gray stone buildings. Green men walked along the streets or rode through the crowds mounted on Ban'thorns, and a number of armed guards stood all around the square, prohibiting the curious from approaching him. There were about fifty guards—enough to cause him trouble even if he were well and free to move.

His weapons, armor, grenades and pouch were all gone. He felt sick and almost hopeless. But deep within him still smoldered the power of the Lens, blended together with an Irish temper that was still fired by thoughts of what the Bi'djar Ri might have done with Mnir'ra. These alone sustained him.

He lay there and thought: First, he had evidently survived what might normally have been a lethal dose of sea water. But what now? Where would he end up? And where would the Serin Ni end up? Were these green men powerful enough in their numbers to recognize a much larger invasion force? Would Djik'ri be able to prepare an adequate resistance? And what about Mnir'ra? Would Gon'ri keep her, or would he try to sacrifice her?

When he turned his head to look at his guards again, he saw a surprising number of spearmen gathering together. They had seen him wake up and were summoning reinforcements. Silently, a whole battalion of them was falling in. And he did not like their looks. But he could only lie there in the best Gulliver tradition and wait for he knew not what to happen.

After a while, a frail green man who wore a dazzling emerald on his forehead came riding into view on a nervous-looking Ban'thorn, and the guards stepped deferentially aside to let him pass. But what startled Gurund Ritroon was the person who rode beside him on a second Ban'thorn. For it was none other than Mnir'ra.

He raised his head and strained at his ropes, but for his pains he received about a dozen spear jabs. None of them penetrated his skin, but he felt that they could have if hard-driven. Mnir'ra tried to spur her mount in his direction, but the guards blocked her path.

"Gurund Ritroon!" she cried out to him. "You should have remained with my people to help them resist the great invasion which is being organized! Gon'ri is gathering all the forces of Bi'djar-Tan against us! And you they intend to sacrifice as a supreme appeal to their gods for vengeance! Oh, Gurund," she cried bitterly, "why did you come?"

The green men were laughing derisively, and the bejeweled one on the Ban'thorn beside Mnir'ra addressed his people, saying, "What delusion is this, calling our prisoner Gurund Ritroon? He is no god, nor could he avenge the death of a *lur'lur*. You see him, do you not? Tied and bound, weakened near to death by the poison of

Ces'son Nar. It is upon such an imposter as this that the redskins have pinned their hopes for victory over us!"

The green men laughed in huge delight, although Gurund Ritroon heard someone remark, aside, to a companion that he was the *only* one who had ever survived the illness that was induced by drinking sea water.

"Mnir'ra," he called to the little queen, "my mission among your people is completed. I have left in Serin-Gor the instruments of vengeance, and Djikn Kinri shall wield them against your enemies. What I have come here for is personal. I have come to take you home!"

While the green men laughed again, Mnir'ra became engaged in conversation with the bejeweled official who had accompanied her. After a moment, she turned hesitantly to Gurund Ritroon and spoke to him.

"This man," she said, "is Kritu Kinri, High Priest of Zich'yeh, the green men's God of Destiny. He is handling most of the government here while Gond'ri's doctors attend his wounds. He says..." She paused, as though she found it difficult to go on.

"Don't be afraid," said Gurund Ritroon. "Let me know the truth. What does this son of a Zat have to say?"

"He says his government will release me if you will demonstrate the use of the weapons you brought with you."

"Where will they release you to, and what are the guarantees?"

THE LITTLE priest quickly conveyed the answer to Mnir'ra, in a low tone of voice, while his beady little eyes never left Gurund Ritroon's face.

"He says," answered Mnir'ra, "that there are enough captured Serin Ni here to man one of their ships and sail it back to Serin-Gor. He says he'll place a ship at their disposal and put me on board, and that you will be allowed to witness our departure."

Gurund Ritroon chose to address Kritu Kinri directly. "My weapons would not do you any good," he said, "because I have left greater ones behind me for the Serin Ni to use against you," He was thinking fast. His statement, which puzzled Mnir'ra inasmuch as it appeared to invalidate his one opportunity for bartering, was carefully calculated to mislead the priest, whom he recognized as a cagey character. If he had immediately agreed, the priest would have suspected a subterfuge, and he would be afforded little opportunity to escape as he would be doubly watched at every turn. Yet, at the same time, by impressing the other of the danger facing their hordes in view of possible new weapons in the hands of the red men, he knew that his own weapons would acquire an even greater value in the eyes of the Bi'djar Ri than before.

Kritu Kinri answered him sharply. "You will leave that matter to us to evaluate. If you refuse to demonstrate your weapons, we will be pleased to sacrifice not only yourself, but Queen Mnir'ra Nikin'ra and all other Serin Ni prisoners simultaneously!"

"One question," said Gurund Ritroon. "When will the second invasion begin?"

Kritu Kinri drew himself up as tall as possible in his saddle. "I am not the one under questioning here!" he retorted.

"All right, all right! I accept the terms! But there is one condition: I cannot effectively demonstrate my weapons in my present weakened condition. I need rest and food. As you can see, I am helplessly weak." Actually, he could have burst his bonds, but his full strength was needed, plus his armament and weapons, before it would be worthwhile risking a break for freedom. Moreover, he was fighting for time—time for Djik'ri, across the Barrier Sea.

Mnir'ra's eyes glistened. "Gurund!" she cried. "I won't leave you here! Let them send the others home, but I will stay!"

She turned to the priest to argue this point, while Gurund Ritroon shouted at her in protest. Suddenly appreciating the true significance of the situation, Kritu Kinri opened his eyes with a new awareness of the possibilities. He nodded to Mnir'ra in silent assent, and then led her away in the direction of the palace...

SO THEY released Gurund Ritroon from his bonds, but they kept him in the great plaza surrounded by a thousand armed guards. He presumed that their respect for him was due largely to a certain amount of superstitious fear that he might be the true Avenger after all. Yet the guards tried to bolster civilian morale by openly defying him and laughing at him. Some even spat at his feet and said he was not fit for sacrifice.

But they gave him food, drink and rest. They thought he might need a week to recover fully, so they gave him three days, and he played the part. Actually, his wonderful resilience restored him within two days.

During this reprieve, he studied his surroundings as unobtrusively as possible. Most outstanding was the fact that the town was built along the base of a great, granite cliff. At one place, above the center of the city, a slender cascade of water descended coldly into a basin below, and Gurund Ritroon wondered if there were some natural reservoir above. He had some ideas if there were, and if he could find out where his weapons were hidden.

He also became familiar with major edifices within the city. One was the palace where Gon'ri the Warrior and Mnir'ra and Kritu Kinri were. It was the stateliest building in sight, with great inlaid domes and decorative towers and pillared facade. But it was not the largest. The temple of Zich'yeh was a spectacular work of stone built to fill worshippers with awe and superstitious fear. Pyramidal steps led up to Grecian-type columns, above which was a colossal carved likeness of the God of Destiny, himself surrounded by gargoyle-like figures representing lesser deities ruled by Zich'yeh. Beyond the columns was an open amphitheater in which were the bloodstained altars, mounted on pyramidal prosceniums and surrounded by burning oil pots which represented eternal fires of faith and devotion.

By the time the third day arrived, Gurund Ritroon was fully his old self, but to safeguard his advantage he acted weak and helpless. He could see preparations getting under way in the harbor for the departure of the shipload of red men. He was determined that Mnir'ra should return to Serin-Gor regardless of her desire to stay, and he sent a message to Kritu Kinri to this effect.

The guards were subsequently ordered to bring him to the palace, and he found that the route lay partially along the water front. In fact, he passed within earshot of the ship carrying the red men and they cheered him.

"Hail, Son of Gur, the Avenger!" they shouted. Gurund Ritroon felt that this was premeditated propaganda intended to confuse and demoralize the green men.

The Bi'djar Ri citizenry were permitted, on the other hand, to belittle him as a simple means of counter-propaganda. They jeered and spat and threw stones. And one small group derisively planted a crown of thorns on his head.

THIS MADE him think hard. And it made him humble—humble before the magnitude of his responsibility. He had told Mnir'ra his mission here was a personal one—that he had done what he could for the Serin Ni. But now he was ashamed. His duties here had only just begun.

Earth belonged to the universe he had left, but the Land of the Lens was a cosmic appendix, an orphan in the scheme of Creation, for which he, by predestination, was responsible. He was forced, once again, to face the inescapable reality that he was Gurund Ritroon. And as he did so, he felt the power of the Lens throbbing in him as never before.

"Do not leave without your queen!" he called out to the Serin Ni. "She will leave with you!"

Many of the red men received the message enthusiastically. They raised their fists and shouted approvingly. But there were some who dissented. One of these latter sprang into the rigging of the ship and called to Gurund Ritroon.

"The Queen cannot come with us," he shouted. "Gon'ri has claimed her in compensation for our resistance to his forces of invasion. If you don't uphold your side of the agreement, he'll have us burned alive on board this ship!" The spokesman was pale with apprehension. There was much grumbling on board, and many an anxious face was turned expectantly upward to Gurund Ritroon's bearded countenance.

"Then go," he answered. "And tell Djikri to try to use everything I taught him!" He could not hope, however, that the greatest weapons, Vee-Nine and Vee-Ten, could be set up by Djik'ri. "Good luck, soldiers! Long live Serin-Gor—and the King!"

As he moved on, under the vicious prodding's of the green men, some of the red men cheered him, while others chanted, "Save us, Mnir'ra, Son of Gur! Hail Gurund Ritroon!"

Then Gurund Ritroon paused to look at something in amazement. Rounding a shoulder of the coastline, there came a great fleet of warships of the green men, which was strange because there was already a considerable fleet in the harbor. Some one hundred and twenty, to be exact. But here came at least a hundred and fifty more, evidently from some other port or ports of Bi'djar-Tan, and they were filled to the gunwhales with powerful painted warriors who carried gigantic bows and arrows longer than themselves. They were green men, but apparently imported from a savage region of the country, for they were a different type. Among them moved excited and vicious-looking Ban'thorns.

"The Djar Li!" shouted many of the guards who were around him, as well as the citizenry. He gathered from excited comments he overheard that the prospect of joining the Second Invasion had made it possible for Gon'ri the Warrior to enlist this fierce, renegade offshoot of the green tribes, and that they were Gra'ghr's most powerful and ferocious fighters.

"Saints preserve us!" Gurund Ritroon muttered, in English. "A fleet of nearly three hundred ships and a floating army of close to thirty thousand—the worst of them being mounted savages!"

He knew that with the right tactics Gon'ri's forces could now penetrate Serin-Gor's improved beach defenses, no matter how well they were reinforced. Unless Vee-Nine and Vee-Ten were set up, Serin-Gor was going to be wiped out!

CHAPTER TEN
Tyrant versus Titan

WITH PREMEDITATED disrespect, the guards prodded Gurund Ritroon into the palace. They led him down a spectacular stone hallway lined with the carved images of leering gods. Then two ornately carved gates swung back, admitting him to the throne room.

A domed ceiling arched above his head. The large room was illuminated by daylight that penetrated cathedral-like niches in the walls. And Gurund Ritroon's heart leaped with exultation when he saw all of his weapons and supplies piled up against the wall to his right. Guarded as they were by the Bi'djar Ri, he felt he could take possession of them when he chose to do so. Then this contempt of the green men was genuine, he thought. They actually did not believe he was Gurund Ritroon. Fools! With the bludgeon alone he could clear out the palace!

On a great stone dais was a granite throne, and on this sat Gon'ri the Warrior—but a greatly altered Gon'ri. His smooth green face of pre-invasion days was now horribly mutilated by burns and white, leprous splotches. One eye was completely gone, removed by surgeons. The other stared glassily at him, entirely lidless. His once impressive countenance had been transformed and twisted into a hideous nightmare, and it did more than hurt his monumental pride. It wounded him mortally, giving him a touch of insanity which was concentrated in a maniacal hatred of the red men.

On Gon'ri's right sat Wur'lun, the *karn-ger* cat, the like of which Gurund Ritroon had never seen. But he stared into its three menacing eyes for only a brief moment, nor was he cognizant of its rumbling growls as it watched him. For on Gon'ri's left sat Mnir'ra.

She was not on a throne. She sat on the floor beside Gon'ri like a slave girl, publicly humiliated. Since Gurund Ritroon had last seen her, she had evidently been subjected to such treatment that her pride had been partially supplanted by fear. There was fear in her eyes as she looked at Gurund Ritroon, and a look of supplication. All of which served to augment his rage, and he had to struggle mightily to control himself.

Gon'ri looked at him in some wonderment for a long moment. Then he addressed him peremptorily. "Whence come you?" he asked.

His attitude suddenly unleashed a reckless defiance in his supposed prisoner. The latter, for the first time since his capture, drew himself to his full height.

"You know as well as I," he replied, in a voice that reverberated in the throne room and made Wur'lun rise to his feet, growling. "I am Son of Gur, the Avenger! I come from the Outer Emptiness, from beyond the Lens, in fulfillment of Gur's ancient promise—that if you disturbed the peace or threatened freedom in this world, I would come, and I would avenge such a violation of the fundamental commandment!"

All other green men in the throne room, even including Kritu Kinri, now looked at Gurund Ritroon in amazement. And Mnir'ra suddenly straightened up with renewed pride.

She looked at him, no longer afraid. But Gon'ri sprang defiantly to his feet.

"You lie!" he shouted. "No god would have been poisoned by the waters of Ces'son Nar, nor would he have permitted himself to be captured! You are an imposter whom I have permitted to live only because I want you to demonstrate the use of your weapons. That demonstration will buy the lives of the Serin Ni whom we hold captive in the harbor, but not your own life. It shall be offered up, with apologies, to Zich'yeh, God of Destiny!"

"And what of Queen Mnir'sr Nikin'ra?" queried Gurund Ritroon serenely.

"That is none of your business!"

GURUND RITROON took several steps toward the throne, while a hundred green bowmen threatened him. "Hear me, Gon'ri," he said in a thunderous voice. "A god may do as he pleases, because his power is superior to that of men. I was not poisoned by Ces'son Nar, nor could your men have tied me down with ropes had I not willed it. I merely chose to come to you in this manner to test you, to learn if you really contemplated total violation of the ancient commandment. Now I am convinced that you are guilty, and I stand ready to avenge!"

"I shall depose here!" shrieked Gon'ri, his single, lidless eye glistening with maniacal rage. "You will do as you are told! I command you to demonstrate the use of your weapons—now!"

"My weapons?" Gurund Ritroon smiled.

"Don't think we are naive," retorted Gon'ri. "Look!" He pointed to the wall of the throne room where the weapons had been.

Now Gurund Ritroon saw that the grenades, the armor, the bludgeon and the crossbow had been moved to one side under a strong guard. The bazooka, however, was mounted in one of the narrow window niches, its muzzle pointing outside. It was bound in this position with rope.

"Outside you will see an ancient stone building," explained Gon'ri. "I am told that the weapon we have mounted in the window has great power. Load it and fire it! Try to destroy that building!"

Gurund Ritroon complied, in part. He walked over to the bazooka and checked it. It was loaded, just as he had left it. Then he looked out the window.

About fifty yards dead ahead a deserted building of stone. But beyond it, at about five hundred yards, towered the pillars of the proud temple of Zich'yeh. And Gurund Ritroon smiled a grim smile.

Deliberately, he elevated the bazooka and fired. There followed a very brief moment of expectant silence. Then, from afar came the roar of an explosion, and observers both inside and outside the palace raised a shout of alarm and dismay as they saw the pillars of the great temple tumble into ruin.

"There is my answer to your threat of sacrifice!" shouted Gurund Ritroon, turning to Gon'ri.

"And here is mine!" cried the latter furiously. Whereupon he released Wur'lun, and the green guards scattered in terror as the tremendous cat darted toward the doomed stranger. Even Mnir'ra rose to her feet and screamed aloud in her fright.

But Gurund Ritroon felt in him the power of the Lens, and he knew that this was the day of the Avenger. The time had come at last to fulfill his ancient destiny.

As the giant animal hurled itself upon him, he felt sudden pain, but he did not yield. He merely concentrated on maneuvering the tremendously powerful creature into a position where he could break its back, which he did. And though it was five or six times as heavy as any green man, he tossed it to the foot of the throne. There were gashes on his arms, legs and abdomen, but his blood coagulated quickly, and he was not seriously harmed. Many bowmen shot arrows at him at point blank range, but the missiles bounced futilely off his skin.

Kritu Kinri leapt to Gon'ri's side and raised his hand. "We are doomed!" he cried. "This is in truth Gurund Ritroon! Lay down your arms!"

But Gon'ri drew his long dagger and plunged it to its hilt into Kritu Kinri. "I am still in command here!" he shouted. "Surround him, spearmen and bowmen! Get in close range! Kill him!"

Gurund Ritroon rushed a wall of spears and a hail of arrows, some of which did penetrate him far enough to be painful. The spears he found he could sweep aside like so many twigs. And many who leapt upon him died.

He wanted his weapons and he got them. The first thing he did was to throw a grenade into the middle of the room. When it went off, it killed a score of Gon'ri's first line infantry who were just entering the throne room to assist the guards. In the resultant confusion he made for the throne and got hold of Mnir'ra. Gon'ri had suddenly disappeared.

"Keep behind me!" he told her. He gave her the grenades to carry.

He had torn the bazooka from its fastenings and now it lay across his back, while in his hands he wielded the bludgeon. The armor he had abandoned, for there was no time to put it on.

HE KNEW that even he could not keep on his feet before the concerted rush of hundreds of armed green men, so he backed toward an exit behind the throne, through which Gon'ri had escaped. With every step he swung the bludgeon, destroying everything that came within its range.

Several guards made the mistake of trying to get behind the pair to capture Mnir'ra. When she cried out in alarm, Gurund Ritroon whirled upon them, decapitating one of them with his club and crushing the chest of another with a blow of his fist. A third guard retreated in terror. Mnir'ra smiled at him proudly. She alone was not awestruck by his terrifying aspect. Death incarnate though he was, she came back to him confidently, and he swept her into his arms and ran through the exit.

Outside, it looked as though the entire nation of the Bidjar Ri was massed against him. The green men were pouring off the great fleets in the harbor and joining the regular troops, jam-packing the whole city. This was all-out war, and he was alone before them.

They were squared off on rooftops behind walls made up of metal shields, their spears and bows poised for action. The spearmen and the bowmen waited, in Bunker Hill fashion, to see the whites of his eyes. But he had no intention of trying to face such overwhelming odds.

He set Mnir'ra down, quickly reloaded his bazooka, and fired into the midst of the heaviest troop concentration he could find. He saw Mnir'ra hide her face to escape the sight of a score of green bodies literally tearing apart and flying through the air in a rain of blood, of metal shields twisted and blasted away like so many leaves blown into dust by the autumn wind, of whole companies of men falling on their faces in terror.

He followed this blast with two grenades, producing equal havoc, and the offensive line became defensive, temporarily retreating. Some warriors were of a tougher strain, however. They deployed themselves in such a way as to corral him against the cliff behind the palace. Beyond these men, Gurund Ritroon saw the more savage Djar Li tribesmen, mounted on shrieking Ban'thorns, coming into the fight with their giant bows and murderous-looking spears. They were yelling a blood-curdling war chant as they drew near, raising the morale of the regulars in the foreground.

Swiftly, Gurund Ritroon led Mnir'ra to the cliff and along its base, until he found a place where he could scale it. He put Mnir'ra on his back and climbed, while arrows pinged against the rocks—the long, swifter arrows of Djar Li, for ordinary arrows could not reach him. Though their power was largely spent when they struck, they struck hard, and he knew that to receive one of these at close range might be very damaging. A close-range volley could perhaps even be fatal.

He climbed faster, getting temporarily out of range. As he withdrew upward, the army closed in below, as much under cover as possible.

When he topped the cliff, he saw what he had hoped to find—a huge natural water reservoir which stretched placidly back among the hills for a quarter of a mile.

"This is going to be good," he said to Mnir'ra, helping her off his back.

"What are you going to do?" she asked excitedly.

"Watch, my love! Just watch!"

He quickly removed all remaining grenades from his knapsack and placed them in a strategic spot at the neck of the waterfall. Then he pulled one of the pins. It was a special grenade he had prepared with a delayed reaction chemical cap. Picking up Mnir'ra, he ran to a granite ledge high above the city of the green men.

"Watch!" he told her. In spite of his excitement, he felt a shiver of delight as he looked down at her lying in his arms. And he wondered if fate would enable him to have her always, or if his strange god-destiny would deprive them both of that happiness.

Mnir'ra sensed something of what he was thinking as he looked down at her. She patted his chest and smiled exactly as every female in the universe has smiled throughout eternity, when she has found her man.

"We may not get back home again," she said, "but to be with you for only a short while is worth death at their hands."

"We'll get back to Serin-Gor, sweetheart," he told her. "Watch the waterfall!"

B-R-R-AM!!!

He felt Mnir'ra stiffen with fright as he watched great segments of the cliff belly out into space, followed by a screen of water. The young avalanche hardly got under way before it was drowned in a flood. A quarter mile lake began to roar out of a great gap in the wall.

The green men below set up a great cry and began to run in every direction in order to get to the highest available points. But the flood caught many and bounced them off their feet onto its crest and then under. It roared and soared between and over the smaller houses, racing in rising tributaries through the streets, overcoming companies and battalions of soldiers and thousands of citizens.

Mnir'ra did not want to see any more. She hid her face against Gurund Ritroon's chest.

Well, he told himself, it was war, wasn't it? The whole planet was at stake. And besides, all was not duck soup yet. These green devils were tough, and the savage Djar Li tribesmen were like the fiends of Pandemonium.

CHAPTER ELEVEN
The Last Invasion

NOW WAS the time to take advantage of the confusion. With Mnir'ra on his back, he descended the cliff swiftly, calculating that the flood was sufficiently spent to wade in, considering his unusual density. With water swirling around his waist, he worked his way through the city, aided by the seaward current, toward the ships that were tugging at their anchors or capsizing in the flood that had obliterated the waterfront.

All he wanted was one ship. As he neared his goal, an arrow or two sang past his ears, and one finally struck him painfully in the shoulder, almost striking Mnir'ra. It was a Djar Li arrow and this time it stuck, but he continued on.

He quickly reached the beach and waded out to a nearby ship. It was a two-masted vessel. Some frantic green men were trying to climb on board but he knocked them off. One, already on board viciously shot a metal-tipped arrow from a captured Serin Ni crossbow, and it grooved his right cheek, drawing blood. The arrow in his shoulder hampered him. He threw his weapons on the ship's deck and climbed aboard, killing the bowman, who dared to grapple with him.

He lay his knapsack and other accoutrements on the deck and also let Mnir'ra down, whereupon he immediately busied himself with the anchor and the sails. Mnir'ra picked up a dead green man's bow and quiver and took up a battle station at the gunwale. Some nearby ships were now swarming with green men, and they too were making ready to sail in pursuit.

"Mnir'ra!" he exclaimed, shoving a black mop of hair off his forehead and wiping his bloody cheek with a forearm. "Get under cover! I'll take care of them!"

He made her take cover in a nearby companionway. When he got up sail on the out-surging flood-tide, he reloaded his bazooka. But he found that he should have looked ahead more frequently than astern after his pursuers. One lone ship came around the promontory. It was a late comer, but it was packed with a hundred painted Djar Li bowmen. Much was their astonishment when they saw the devastation wrought in the capital city and when they saw also the spectacular cause of it all sailing out to sea with his back toward them.

The pursuing crews saw the newcomer and at once realized the magnitude of their advantage. As though by mutual consent, no signal of recognition was given to the other ship. The commander of the new ship cautioned his men to absolute silence.

Gurund Ritroon sensed that something was wrong, but he turned too late. It was lucky, in fact, that he did not turn fully around before they fired at such close range, for he might have been blinded by the hail of long, hard-flung arrows. He got them in his back and right side. About eight arrows twanged into his hide to a depth of from a quarter inch to three inches, filling him with insupportable agony. His mind blacked out momentarily, and he sagged to his knees while the green men cheered.

The triumphant bowmen reached for more arrows while scores of other ships near shore filled their sails and began to move toward him.

"Gurund!" cried Mnir'ra from the companionway. "They're going to shoot again!"

GRITTING his teeth, he raised his bazooka horizontal with the water and fired. The resultant explosion put the aggressor ship out of commission, with one mast down and a hole in its side, listing to port. To show he meant business, he loaded and fired again, and the blast threw many of the crew into the sky.

This was a lesson for the following ships, although they did not know that the Avenger was out of ammunition. They kept their distance. They only followed now because they were hopeful that the blast of arrows he had received would prove fatal.

As Gurund Ritroon sank lower on the deck in a bloody sweat, he saw that about a hundred and seventy of Gon'ri's ships had formed into a formidable vengeance fleet and had gotten under way. That was still an ample force to take Serin-Gor, even against fire brands and catapults and crossbows.

Mnir'ra came to him where he lay panting on the deck. She bent over his face with a pale, frightened look. "Don't be afraid, honey," he spoke unconvincingly. "We'll make it yet."

"Gurund!" she answered. "The Bi'djar Ri mean nothing to me! It is you! Only you. You are losing blood! I must do something for you. Have you some medicine in your things? May I pull out the arrows?"

"First," he panted weakly, "you'd better learn something about navigation and how to steer home in case I'm unable to help."

The yellow suns of Gra'ghr were sinking, and he pointed out the rising purple moon that would be the road marker on the way back to Serin-Gor. The wind, he knew, was constant, almost unvarying, out here on the poisonous Barrier Sea. He told her to concentrate on the helm.

"Now you can try pulling out some of the arrows, while she's sailing easy," he said. "It'll hurt least if you'll use both hands on the arrows and pull them out quickly."

To Mnir'ra it was equally as painful. But she went to her task, while Gurund Ritroon bit his lip and tried to think hard of something else, of Djik'ri and his preparations against this new invasion.

On the third arrow he could not resist crying out, but Mnir'ra knew it was then or never and she continued swiftly, while his head swam. When she finished, he said feebly, "How far back is the fleet?"

"They stay always at the same distance," she answered.

He drifted into an exhausted stupor. Too much blood, he thought disconnectedly. Weakening…

HE AWOKE to find Mnir'ra's face and hair pressed against his cheek. She was crying.

"Beloved," he whispered.

"Oh, dearest! You're dying!" she cried helplessly. "What can I do? I love you so, and I am so helpless. And I need you—oh my darling, I need you. This whole world needs you! You can't die!"

"I'm still ticking," he said, forcing a grin. He was aware of a feverish glow in his face. He was not very hopeful. "If something happens to me," he said, "tell Djik'ri to make use of everything I taught him."

But he thought that all he had taught Djik'ri would come to nothing if the green men took over, or it would be used wrongly. It was more than a Promethean knowledge of fire. He thought in desperation that he would have to survive long enough to set up Vee Ten and Vee Eleven. Without these the red men were lost.

With only the purple moon to light the sky, the Barrier Sea presented a weird, unreal aspect. The numerous sails of Gon'ri's super invasion fleet filled the horizon like motionless ghosts frozen in eternity. And somehow Gurund Ritroon felt that this was his last night on Gra'ghr.

But Mnir'ra's soft cheek against his was real. She kissed him lingeringly and told him many womanly things that he could not consciously grasp but which he felt instinctively were everything he wanted to hear.

"You must live," she whispered, caressing his ear with her lips. "If you die, I will walk in Zi'lgar-Lon alone, I will follow Altinra into the sleep of forever, for I cannot live with only the memory of you!"

He caressed her, in spite of his pain, and he kissed her mouth, her throat, and her breast.

"I've looked for you for a million years," he gasped, "but now I may lose you, I may be taken back through the Lens. If the Lens takes me—" Pain stopped his voice.

"If the Lens takes you, you will try to return," she said.

"I—I don't know," he answered. "Maybe—"

"You must promise!" she exclaimed.

"But maybe I can't!" he protested. "The Lens—"

"I shall wait," she said. "A hundred purple moons I shall wait—if you go. After that—I shall walk where Altinra walked, in Zi'lgar-Lon."

"Mnir'ra."

"Yes, beloved?"

He clenched his teeth against pain and took her tightly into his arms...

DAWN FOUND him half delirious, within sight of Serin-Gor, and with Gon'ri's great fleet almost within bow range. They were gaining confidence, because their lookouts had not seen him get to his feet once during the trip.

Mnir'ra climbed to the crow's nest and reported to him what she saw. The catapults on shore were three times as numerous as before, all set and ready. Crude forts made out of sand bags and logs had been set up all along the beach, and she could see what seemed to be as many as ten thousand men with shields waiting for the great invasion.

The fact that nobody was cheering the approach of their own ship led her to believe that her countrymen considered theirs as the flagship of the enemy.

"Gon'ri is within bow range," she said, "but we are not yet in range of our own archers."

He feebly lifted his head and he thought it would split with the effort. "Unless they get Vee Ten set up in time, they're still lost! I've got to hold out! We've got to get there, Mnir'ra—ahead of Bi'djar Ri!"

But Gon'ri's hard driving fleet drew ever closer on their heels and Mnir'ra saw with dread the endless number of Djar Li bowmen pressed against the gunwales, all their cruel little eyes turned upon Gurund Ritroon.

"Done for! Done for!" he panted, under his breath, in English, trying to keep his head up so that he could see the shore.

Suddenly, a vast shower of arrows came at him, and he cried out to Mnir'ra to duck down in the crow's nest. But when she saw more arrows dart into his body, she merely stood where she was, eyes wide and dry. The feeling that he would be killed a certainty in her heart.

"Mnir'ra!" he shouted. "Protect yourself! You'll be killed!"

Just then they both saw it. They looked and were silent with astonishment. Out from shore sped Vee Ten, sure and terrible, a streak of guaranteed death.

But Gurund Ritroon had no time to be elated over the apparent fact that Djik'ri had actually set up Vee Ten himself. Because Vee Ten happened to be aimed straight at his own ship!

The rocket bomb soared in an arc and headed on a chute of flame directly for the deck. In a fit of desperation, he found one last hidden store of energy, enough to help him stagger to his feet.

FROM THE shore, Djik'ri and his men looked aghast at the sight of their own Avenger rising up off the deck and taking the full blast of the bomb. His chest and face were hidden in a roaring blast that caused the ship to rock violently. Then he was seen to fall to the deck, while the figure of Serin-Gor's lost queen, Mnir'sr Nikin'ra, was seen to climb frantically down from the crow's nest.

Djik'ri, from his vantage point behind the rocket bomb batteries, choked on a cry of anguish.

"It's Gurund Ritroon and the Queen!" cried a lieutenant at his side. "Great Gur! We've destroyed the Avenger!"

"Sink the fleet!" shouted Djik'ri bitterly. "Sink them all! Give them everything we've got! Vee Ten! The catapults! The fire brands! Pray Gur that Mnir'ra's ship doesn't strike a Vee Eleven!"

Little did Mnir'ra know that her ship was wallowing crazily along between dark blobs of death hidden in the water—mines fashioned by Gurund Ritroon's own hands.

She was only vaguely aware of a sky filled with flaming death, of ships blasting into pieces of wood and men, sails rising in flames from the fire brands. For Gurund Ritroon, her great, benevolent avenger god, was dying. She stood straight and motionlessly for a moment beside him and looked with almost unseeing eyes out at the battle. She felt the imminence of death upon her own head as the hard driving enemy ships closed in around her. But death seemed not unwelcome. She kneeled suddenly and laid her small head on her lover's brow. For a moment, she thought he stirred. A smile formed faintly on his bloodied lips.

Then she straightened up again, vividly aware of a ship next to hers and a green man with horrible scars marking his one-eyed face. He stood on the bridge with a Serin Ni crossbow in his powerful hands. And its metal-barbed arrow was aimed at her heart.

She could sense the wave of triumphant hate that Gon'ri the Warrior's single, staring eye sent out. She stood unyielding where she was, a perfect target.

At that moment, however, Vee Eleven abruptly entered the picture. Both ships struck the mine simultaneously. Blast knocked them ponderously apart, tearing up planking and rigging and dumping green men into the sea. And it knocked Gurund Ritroon into fitful consciousness.

He was in the water. He saw Mnir'ra swimming like a mermaid, and he remembered with a great sense of relief that she was one of Gra'ghr's greatest swimmers. But his bodily density was carrying him swiftly downward.

His perspective became confused. Was he hurtling through water—or endless space?

LOUISE HAD long since ceased to cry. She sat motionlessly beside the hospital bed and just listened to Flannigan as he droned onward, trying to finish his insane story. His eyes stared beyond her, as though looking again into his imagined Land of the Lens.

"You know most of the rest," he said. "When I came back out of Rheingold crater, Deegan and your father were still there. Gilbert had been struck down by a meteor. Although I had lived many moons in the Land of the Lens, in our own time only seventy hours had passed.

"And so we started back, I went along merely because I felt I owed it to them, to get them back to Earth if I could. But you know about that—our struggle against the meteors, and the radioactive infections picked up on the moon. Deegan died only one day from home, and now your father—"

"And you, Michael!" she cried out, her eyes flooding again with tears.

"No," he said. "I may live."

Her face brightened, hopefully. "What do you mean? How, Michael?"

"If I can get back through the Lens," he said. "The Lens won't let me die if I am within its range of direct influence. It will take me through! I've figured that out. I'm quite sure of it!"

She shook her head, shuddering, and turned away to hide her face.

"You think I'm insane," he said swiftly. "You think the Land of the Lens is the product of delirium, induced by my experiences and my illness. But I was there, and I'm going back! I've got to!"

Louise turned to him and threw her arms about his neck, sobbing against him. "Oh, darling, I dreamed of our love and our life together—here! If you are to live, why can't you stay—"

"You forget. Here I'm dying of radioactive poisoning, and I'm sterile, in case you don't remember. But if I could get back through the Lens—"

"Oh Michael! Michael!" she sobbed.

"Louise, you're young, healthy and beautiful. Your life is before you. Would you want me to stay on here and die? What good would that do either of us?"

"But Michael! This seemingly mad dream of going back to the Moon—how could you? The expedition you made cost millions of dollars. It's all over. Nobody is going to refinance—"

"Wrong again, sweet. You forget that they want the rest of those readings from outer space. The ship still exists. Nobody would volunteer to pilot it, because it means practical suicide. But to me, an otherwise doomed man, it means a slim chance for life—endless life. Science may be willing to finance repairs to that ship, and a load of fuel—enough fuel for a one-way trip, anyway. I'll pay them for it. I'll radio back the readings they want…"

TWO MONTHS later, Louise was driving home from Mount Palomar. They had permitted her to see the rocket herself, a tiny pinpoint of light, far out in the depths of space.

True to his word, Flannigan had sent back more readings from the new instruments, until meteors had struck, destroying his transmitter. After that, she could only guess at his fate.

But she could not help wondering, as she drove along over the highway, if there was actually a Land of the Lens, and if he would make it after all. And if he returned there, would it be as god or man? If he was too late and Mnir'sr Nikinra had already gone to Zi'lgar-Lon, would he follow her?

She shook her head, trying to regain a foothold in the rational world of her own terra firma. It was all so insane. There was no Lens, she told herself, no Gra'ghr, no Serin-Gor.

But into her mind crept a vision of a lonely, bewhiskered space pilot, his eyes glued to his periscope, maneuvering a badly battered and leaking ship desperately toward his goal.

And she heard faintly the exotic strains of an unearthly song, words that perhaps Flannigan himself was listening to, or singing, even now…

> *Why, my love, is fate so cold,*
> *To fill the heart in vain,*
> *Giving today to have and hold,*
> *Only to lose again?*
> *Meaning dies and beauty's left*
> *Alone in desert's waste,*
> *O leave me not of thee bereft!*
> *I follow thee in haste!*

THE END

If you've enjoyed this book, you will not want to miss these terrific titles…

If you've enjoyed this book, you will not want to miss these terrific titles…

ARMCHAIR SCI-FI & HORROR DOUBLE NOVELS, $12.95 each

D-101 **THE CONQUEST OF THE PLANETS** by John W. Campbell
THE MAN WHO ANNEXED THE MOON by Bob Olsen

D-102 **WEAPON FROM THE STARS** by Rog Phillips
THE EARTH WAR by Mack Reynolds

D-103 **THE ALIEN INTELLIGENCE** by Jack Williamson
INTO THE FOURTH DIMENSION by Ray Cummings

D-104 **THE CRYSTAL PLANETOIDS** by Stanton A. Coblentz
SURVIVORS FROM 9,000 B. C. by Robert Moore Williams

D-105 **THE TIME PROJECTOR** by David H. Keller, M.D. and David Lasser
STRANGE COMPULSION by Philip Jose Farmer

D-106 **WHOM THE GODS WOULD SLAY** by Paul W. Fairman
MEN IN THE WALLS by William Tenn

D-107 **LOCKED WORLDS** by Edmond Hamilton
THE LAND THAT TIME FORGOT by Edgar Rice Burroughs

D-108 **STAY OUT OF SPACE** by Dwight V. Swain
REBELS OF THE RED PLANET by Charles L. Fontenay

D-109 **THE METAMORPHS** by S. J. Byrne
MICROCOSMIC BUCCANEERS by Harl Vincent

D-110 **YOU CAN'T ESCAPE FROM MARS** by E. K. Jarvis
THE MAN WITH FIVE LIVES by David V. Reed

ARMCHAIR SCIENCE FICTION CLASSICS, $12.95 each

C-34 **30 DAY WONDER**
by Richard Wilson

C-35 **G.O.G. 666**
by John Taine

C-36 **RALPH 124C 41+**
by Hugo Gernsback

ARMCHAIR SCI-FI & HORROR GEMS SERIES, $12.95 each

G-11 **SCIENCE FICTION GEMS, Vol. Six**
Edmond Hamilton and others

G-12 **HORROR GEMS, Vol. Six**
H. P. Lovecraft and others

If you've enjoyed this book, you will not want to miss these terrific titles...

If you've enjoyed this book, you will not want to miss these terrific titles...

ARMCHAIR MYSTERY & SCIENCE FICTION CLASSICS
$12.95 each

C-40   **MODEL FOR MURDER**
by Stephen Marlowe

C-41   **PRELUDE TO MURDER**
by Sterling Noel

C-42   **DEAD WEIGHT**
by Frank Kane

C-43   **A DAME CALLED MURDER**
by Milton Ozaki

C-44   **THE GREATEST ADVENTURE**
by John Taine

C-45   **THE EXILE OF TIME**
by Ray Cummings

C-46   **STORM OVER WARLOCK**
by Andre Norton

C-47   **MAN OF MANY MINDS**
by E. Everett Evans

C-48   **THE GODS OF MARS**
by Edgar Rice Burroughs

C-49   **BRIGANDS OF THE MOON**
by Ray Cummings

C-50   **SPACE HOUNDS OF IPC**
by E. E. "Doc" Smith

C-51   **THE LANI PEOPLE**
by J. F. Bone

C-52   **THE MOON POOL**
by A. Merritt

C-53   **IN THE DAYS OF THE COMET**
by H. G. Wells

C-54   **TRIPLANETARY**
E. E. Doc Smith

If you've enjoyed this book, you will not want to miss these terrific titles...

ARMCHAIR SCI-FI & HORROR DOUBLE NOVELS, $12.95 each

D-121 **THE GENIUS BEASTS** by Frederik Pohl
THIS WORLD IS TABOO by Murray Leinster

D-122 **THE COSMIC LOOTERS** by Edmond Hamilton
WANDL THE INVADER by Ray Cummings

D-123 **ROBOT MEN OF BUBBLE CITY** by Rog Phillips
DRAGON ARMY by William Morrison

D-124 **LAND BEYOND THE LENS** by S. J. Byrne
DIPLOMAT-AT-ARMS by Keith Laumer

D-125 **VOYAGE OF THE ASTEROID, THE** by Laurence Manning
REVOLT OF THE OUTWORLDS by Milton Lesser

D-126 **OUTLAW IN THE SKY** by Chester S. Geier
LEGACY FROM MARS by Raymond Z. Gallun

D-127 **THE GREAT FLYING SAUCER INVASION** by Geoff St. Reynard
THE BIG TIME by Fritz Leiber

D-128 **MIRAGE FOR PLANET X** by Stanley Mullen
POLICE YOUR PLANET by Lester del Rey

D-129 **THE BRAIN SINNERS** by Alan E. Nourse
DEATH FROM THE SKIES by A. Hyatt Verrill

D-139 **CRY CHAOS** by Dwight V. Swain
THE DOOR THROUGH SPACE By Marion Zimmer Bradley

ARMCHAIR SCIENCE FICTION CLASSICS, $12.95 each

C-55 **UNDER THE TRIPLE SUNS**
by Stanton A. Coblentz

C-56 **STONE FROM THE GREEN STAR**
by Jack Williamson

C-57 **ALIEN MINDS**
by E. Everett Evans

ARMCHAIR MASTERS OF SCIENCE FICTION SERIES, $16.95 each

G-13 **SCIENCE FICTION GEMS, Vol. Seven**
Jack Vance and others

G-14 **HORROR GEMS, Vol. Seven**
Robert Bloch and others

ON THE VERGE OF INTERPLANETARY WAR

Retief had just one job on the planet Northroyal—to save the galaxy from total madness and a long, destructive war. But unfortunately his assignment verged on the suicidal. It was a mission so intricate, so desperate, that its chance of success was practically nil. Not only would he have to use bravado, belligerence, and wit to bully his way through the planet's lower echelons of power, but his aging body would also be put to the ultimate tests of physical combat; and if successful, he would find himself in the unenviable position of being tried as a traitor and executed. So with a frayed cloak and an old horse and a packet in his saddlebags— not to mention blood, guts, and brains—he set out to meet his destiny.

Join science fiction master Keith Laumer as he spins a remarkable, nailing-biting tale of interplanetary intrigue.

CAST OF
CHARACTERS

RETIEF
The job of this aging diplomat was a desperate one, yet simple: walk into a lion's den and single-handedly tame the beast of war.

FITZRAVEN
This young squire was energetic and loyal, even if he did have suspicions about his new master's true identity.

THE CHAMPION
He was a simple street merchant, but in the arena there was no one who could best him. Well…almost no one.

EMPEROR ROLAN
As the Emperor of Northroyal, he was determined to bring his planet back into prominence—by force if necessary.

PRINCESS MONICA
She was a dark beauty, and a princess of the royal line. But her ascension to even higher power was something of a surprise.

MAGNAN
Retief was a thorn in his side. So what better way to rid himself of an irritant than to send him on a suicide mission.

THE BATTLE ENSIGN
He knew enough about the ancient codes not to be swayed by the bullying of higher officials—a fact that would save Retief's life.

DIPLOMAT-AT-ARMS

By
KEITH LAUMER

ARMCHAIR FICTION
PO Box 4369, Medford, Oregon 97504

*For more information about Armchair Books and products, visit our
website at...*

www.armchairfiction.com

Or email us at...

armchairfiction@yahoo.com

CHAPTER ONE

THE cold white sun of Northroyal glared on pale dust and vivid colors in the narrow raucous street. Retief rode slowly, unconscious of the huckster's shouts, the kaleidoscope of smells, the noisy milling crowd. His thoughts were on events of long ago on distant worlds; thoughts that set his features in narrow-eyed grimness. His bony, powerful horse, unguided, picked his way carefully, with flaring nostrils, wary eyes alert in the turmoil.

The mount sidestepped a darting gamin and Retief leaned forward, patted the sleek neck. The job had some compensations, he thought; it was good to sit on a fine horse again, to shed the gray business suit...

A dirty-faced man pushed a fruit cart almost under the animal's head; the horse shied, knocked over the cart. At once a muttering crowd began to gather around the heavy-shouldered gray-haired man. He reined in and sat scowling, an ancient brown cape over his shoulders, a covered buckler slung at the side of the worn saddle, a scarred silver-worked claymore strapped across his back in the old cavalier fashion.

Retief hadn't liked this job when he had first heard of it. He had gone alone on madmans' errands before, but that had been long ago—a phase of his career that should have been finished. And the information he had turned up in his background research had broken his professional detachment. Now the locals were trying an old tourist game on him; ease the outlander into a spot, then demand money…

Well, Retief thought, this was as good a time as any to start playing the role; there was a hell of a lot here in the quaint city of Fragonard that needed straightening out.

"Make way, you rabble!" he roared suddenly, "or by the chains of the sea-god I'll make a path through you!" He spurred the horse; neck arching, the mount stepped daintily forward.

The crowd made way reluctantly before him. "Pay for the merchandise you've destroyed," called a voice.

"Let peddlers keep a wary eye for their betters," snorted the man loudly, his eye roving over the faces before him. A tall fellow with long yellow hair stepped squarely into his path.

"There are no rabble or peddlers here," he said angrily. "Only true cavaliers of the Clan Imperial…"

The mounted man leaned from his saddle to stare into the eyes of the other. His seamed brown face radiated scorn. "When did a true cavalier turn to commerce? If you were trained to the Code you'd know a gentleman doesn't soil his hands with penny-grubbing, and that the Emperor's highroad belongs to the mounted knight. So clear your rubbish out of my path, if you'd save it."

"Climb down off that nag," shouted the tall young man, reaching for the bridle. "I'll show you some practical knowledge of the Code. I challenge you to stand and defend yourself."

In an instant the thick barrel of an antique Imperial Guards power gun was in the gray-haired man's hand. He leaned negligently on the high pommel of his saddle with his left elbow, the pistol laid across his forearm pointing unwaveringly at the man before him.

The hard old face smiled grimly. "I don't soil my hands in street brawling with new hatched nobodies," he said. He nodded toward the arch spanning the street ahead. "Follow me through the arch, if you call yourself a man and a Cavalier." He moved on then; no one hindered him. He rode in silence through the crowd, pulled up at the gate barring the street. This would be the first real test of his cover identity. The papers that had gotten him through Customs and Immigration at Fragonard Spaceport the day before had been burned along with the civilian clothes. From here on he'd be getting by on the uniform and a cast-iron nerve.

A purse-mouthed fellow wearing the uniform of a Lieutenant-Ensign in the Household Escort Regiment looked him over, squinted his eyes, smiled sourly.

"What can I do for you, Uncle?" He spoke carelessly, leaning against the engraved buttress mounting the wrought-iron gate. Yellow and green sunlight filtered down through the leaves of the giant linden trees bordering the cobbled street.

The gray-haired man stared down at him. "The first thing you can do, Lieutenant Ensign," he said in a voice of cold steel, "is come to a position of attention."

The thin man straightened, frowning. "What's that?" His expression hardened. "Get down off that beast and let's have a look at your papers—if you've got any."

The mounted man didn't move. "I'm making allowances for the fact that your regiment is made up of idlers who've never learned to soldier," he said quietly. "But having had your attention called to it, even you should recognize the insignia of a Battle Commander."

The officer stared, glancing over the drab figure of the old man. Then he saw the tarnished gold thread worked into the design of a dragon rampant, almost invisible against the faded color of the heavy velvet cape.

He licked his lips, cleared his throat, hesitated. What in name of the Tormented One would a top-ranking battle officer be doing on this thin old horse, dressed in plain worn clothing? "Let me see your papers—Commander," he said.

The Commander flipped back the cape to expose the ornate butt of the power pistol.

"Here are my credentials," he said. "Open the gate."

"Here," the Ensign spluttered. "What's this…"

"For a man who's taken the Emperor's commission," the old man said, "you're criminally ignorant of the courtesies due a general officer. Open the gate or I'll blow it open. You'll not deny the way to an Imperial Battle officer." He drew the pistol.

The Ensign gulped, thought fleetingly of sounding the alarm signal, of insisting on seeing papers… Then as the pistol came up, he closed the switch, and the gate swung open. The heavy hooves of the gaunt horse clattered past him; he caught a glimpse of a small brand on the lean flank. Then he was staring after the retreating back of the terrible old man, Battle Commander indeed! The old fool was wearing a fortune in valuable antiques, and the animal bore the brand of a thoroughbred battle-horse. He'd better report this… He picked up the communicator, as a tall young man with an angry face came up to the gate.

RETIEF rode slowly down the narrow street lined with the stalls of suttlers, metalsmiths, weapons technicians, freelance squires. The first obstacle was behind him. He hadn't played it very suavely, but he had been in no mood for bandying words. He had been angry ever since he had started this job; and that, he told himself, wouldn't do. He was beginning to regret his high-handedness with the crowd outside the gate. He should save the temper for those responsible, not the bystanders, and in any event, an agent of the Corps should stay cool at all times. That was essentially the same criticism that Magnan had handed him along with the assignment, three months ago.

"The trouble with you, Retief," Magnan had said, "is that you are unwilling to accept the traditional restraints of the Service; you conduct yourself too haughtily, too much in the manner of a free agent…"

His reaction, he knew, had only proved the accuracy of his superior's complaint. He should have nodded penitent agreement, indicated that improvement would be striven for earnestly; instead, he had sat expressionless, in a silence that inevitably appeared antagonistic.

He remembered how Magnan had moved uncomfortably, cleared his throat, and frowned at the papers before him. "Now, in the matter of your next assignment," he said, "we have a serious situation to deal with in an area that could be critical."

Retief almost smiled at the recollection. The man had placed himself in an amusing dilemma. It was necessary to emphasize the great importance of the job at hand, and simultaneously to avoid letting Retief have the satisfaction of feeling that he was to be entrusted with anything vital; to express the lack of confidence the Corps felt in him while at the same time invoking his awareness of the great trust he was receiving. It was strange how Magnan could rationalize his personal dislike into a righteous concern for the best interests of the Corps.

Magnan had broached the nature of the assignment obliquely, mentioning his visit as a tourist to Northroyal, a charming, backward little planet settled by Cavaliers, refugees from the breakup of the Empire of the Lily.

Retief knew the history behind Northroyal's tidy, proud, tradition-bound society. When the Old Confederation broke up, dozens of smaller governments had grown up among the civilized worlds. For a time, the Lily Empire had been among the most vigorous of them, comprising Twenty-one worlds, and supporting an excellent military force under the protection of which the Lilyan merchant fleet had carried trade to a thousand far-flung worlds.

When the Concordiat had come along, organizing the previously sovereign states into a new Galactic jurisdiction, the Empire of the Lily had resisted, and had for a time held the massive Concordiat fleets at bay. In the end, of course, the gallant but outnumbered Lilyan forces had been driven back to the gates of the home world. The planet of Lily had been saved catastrophic bombardment only by a belated truce which guaranteed self-determination to Lily on the cessation of hostilities, disbandment of the Lilyan fleet, and the exile of the entire membership of the Imperial Suite, which, under the Lilyan clan tradition, had numbered over ten thousand individuals. Every man, woman, and child who could claim even the most distant blood relationship to the Emperor, together with their servants, dependents, retainers, and protégés, were included. The move took weeks to complete, but at the end of it the Cavaliers, as they were known, had been transported to an uninhabited, cold, sea-world, which they named Northroyal. A popular bit of lore in connection with the exodus had it that the ship bearing the Emperor himself had slipped away en route to exile, and that the ruler had sworn that he would not return until the day he could come with an army of liberation. He had never been heard from again.

The land area of the new world, made up of innumerable islands, totaled half a million square miles. Well stocked with basic supplies and equipment, the cavaliers had set to work and turned their rocky fief into a snug, well integrated—if tradition ridden—society, and today exported seafoods, fine machinery, and tourist literature.

It was in the latter department that Northroyal was best known. Tales of the pomp and color, the quaint inns and good food, the beautiful girls, the brave display of royal cavalry, and the fabulous annual Tournament of the Lily attracted a goodly number of sightseers, and the Cavalier Line was now one of the planet's biggest foreign-exchange earners.

Magnan had spoken of Northroyal's high industrial potential, and her well-trained civilian corps of space navigators.

"The job of the Corps," Retief interrupted, "is to seek out and eliminate threats to the peace of the Galaxy. How does a little storybook world like Northroyal get into the act?"

"More easily than you might imagine," Magnan said. "Here you have a close-knit society, proud, conscious of a tradition of military power, empire. A clever rabble-rouser using the right appeal would step into a ready-made situation there. It would take only an order on the part of the planetary government to turn the factories to war production, and convert the merchant fleet into a war fleet—and we'd be faced with a serious power imbalance—a storm center."

"I think you're talking nonsense, Mr. Minister," Retief said bluntly. "They've got more sense than that. They're not so far gone on tradition as to destroy themselves. They're a practical people."

Magnan drummed his fingers on the desk top. "There's one factor I haven't covered yet," he said. "There has been what amounts to a news blackout from Northroyal during the last six months…"

Retief snorted. "What news?"

Magnan had been enjoying the suspense. "Tourists have been having great difficulty getting to Northroyal," he said. "Fragonard, the capital, is completely closed to outsiders. We managed, however, to get an agent in." He paused, gazing at Retief. "It seems," he went on, "that the rightful Emperor has turned up."

Retief narrowed his eyes. "What's that?" he said sharply.

Magnan drew back, intimidated by the power of Retief's tone, annoyed by his own reaction. In his own mind, Magnan was candid enough to know that this was the real basis for his intense dislike for his senior agent. It was an instinctive primitive fear of physical violence. Not that Retief had ever assaulted anyone; but he had an air of mastery that made Magnan feel trivial.

"The Emperor," Magnan repeated. "The traditional story is that he was lost on the voyage to Northroyal. There was a legend that he had slipped out of the hands of the Concordiat in order to gather new support for a counteroffensive, hurl back the invader, all that sort of thing."

"The Concordiat collapsed of its own weight within a century," Retief said. "There's no invader to hurl back. Northroyal is free and independent like every other world."

"Of course, of course," Magnan said. "But you're missing the emotional angle, Retief. It's all very well to be independent; but what about the dreams of Empire, the vanished glory, destiny, et cetera!"

"What about them?"

"That's all our agent heard; it's everywhere. The news strips are full of it. Video is playing it up; everybody's talking it. The returned Emperor seems to be a clever propagandist; the next step will be a full scale mobilization. And we're not equipped to handle that."

"What am I supposed to do about all this?"

"Your orders are, and I quote, to proceed to Fragonard and there employ such measures as shall be appropriate to negate the present trend toward an expansionist sentiment among the populace." Magnan passed a document across the desk to Retief for his inspection.

CHAPTER TWO

THE ORDERS were brief, and wasted no wordage on details. As an officer of the Corps with the rank of Counselor, Retief enjoyed wide latitude, with broad powers—and corresponding responsibility in the event of failure. Retief wondered how this assignment had devolved on him, among the thousands of Corps agents scattered through the Galaxy. Why was one man being handed a case that, on the face of it, should call for a full mission?

"This looks like quite an undertaking for a single agent, Mr. Minister," Retief said.

"Well, of course, if you don't feel you can handle it..." Magnan looked solemn.

Retief looked at him, smiling faintly, Magnan's tactics had been rather obvious. Here was one of those nasty jobs that could easily pass in reports as routine if all went well; but even a slight mistake could mean complete failure, and failure meant war; and the agent who had let it happen would be finished in the Corps.

There was danger in the scheme for Magnan, too. The blame might reflect back on him. Probably he had plans for averting disaster after Retief had given up. He was too shrewd to leave himself out in the open. And for that matter, Retief reflected, too good an agent to let the situation get out of hand.

No, it was merely an excellent opportunity to let Retief discredit himself, with little risk of any great credit accruing to him in the remote event of success.

Retief could, of course, refuse the assignment, but that would be the end of his career. He would never be advanced to the rank of Minister, and age limitations would force his retirement in a year or two. That would be an easy victory for Magnan.

Retief liked his work as an officer-agent of the Diplomatic Corps, that ancient supranational organization dedicated to the contravention of war. He had made his decision long ago, and he had learned to accept his life as it was, with all its imperfections. It was easy enough to complain about the petty intrigues, the tyrannies of rank, the small inequities. But these were merely a part of the game, another challenge to be met and dealt with. The overcoming of obstacles was Jame Retief's specialty. Some of the obstacles were out in the open, the recognized difficulties inherent in any tough assignment. Others were concealed behind a smoke-screen of personalities and efficiency reports; and both were equally important. You did your job in the field, and then you threaded your way through the maze of Corps politics. And if you couldn't handle the job—any part of it—you'd better find something else to do.

He had accepted the assignment of course, after letting Magnan wonder for a few minutes; and then for two months he had buried himself in research, gathering every scrap of information, direct and indirect, that the massive files of the Corps would yield. He had soon found himself immersed in the task, warming to its challenge, fired with emotions ranging from grief to rage as he ferreted out the hidden pages in the history of the exiled Cavaliers.

He had made his plan, gathered a potent selection of ancient documents and curious objects; a broken chain of gold, a tiny key, a small silver box. And now he was here, inside the compound of the Grand Corrida.

Everything here in these ways surrounding and radiating from the Field of the Emerald Crown—the arena itself—was devoted to the servicing and supplying of the thousands of First Day contenders in the Tournament of the Lily, and the housing and tending of the dwindling number of winners who stayed on for the following days. There were tiny eating places, taverns, inns; all consciously antique in style, built in imitation of their counterparts left behind long ago on far off Lily.

"Here you are, pop, first-class squire," called a thin red-haired fellow.

"Double up and save credits," called a short dark man. "First-day contract…"

Shouts rang back and forth across the alley-like street as the stall keepers scented a customer. Retief ignored them, moved on toward the looming wall of the arena. Ahead, a slender youth stood with folded arms before his stall, looking toward the approaching figure on the black horse. He leaned forward, watching Retief intently, then straightened, turned and grabbed up a tall narrow body shield from behind him. He raised the shield over his head, and as Retief came abreast, called "Battle officer!"

Retief reined in the horse and looked down at the youth.

"At your service, sir," the young man said. He stood straight and looked Retief in the eye, Retief looked back. The horse minced, tossed his head.

"What is your name, boy?" Retief asked.

"Fitzraven, sir."

"Do you know the Code?"

"I know the Code, sir."

Retief stared at him, studying his face, his neatly cut uniform of traditional imperial green, the old but well-oiled leather of his belt and boots.

"Lower your shield, Fitzraven," he said. "You're engaged." He swung down from his horse. "The first thing I want is care for my mount. His name is Danger-by-Night. And then I want an inn for myself."

"I'll care for the horse myself, Commander," Fitzraven said. "And you will find good lodging at the sign of the Phoenix-in-Dexter-Chief—quarters are held ready for my client." The squire took the bridle, pointing toward the inn a few doors away.

TWO HOURS later, Retief came back to the stall, a thirty-two ounce steak and a bottle of Neauveau Beaujolais having satisfied a monumental appetite induced by the long ride down from the spaceport north of Fragonard. The plain banner he had carried in his saddlebag fluttered now from the staff above the stall. He moved through the narrow room to a courtyard behind, and stood in the doorway watching as Fitzraven curried the dusty hide of the lean black horse. The saddle and fittings were laid out on a heavy table, ready for cleaning. There was clean straw in the stall where the horse stood, and an empty grain bin and water bucket indicated the animal had been well fed and watered.

Retief nodded to the squire, and strolled around the courtyard staring up at the deep blue sky of early evening above the irregular line of roofs and chimneys, noting the other squires, the variegated mounts stabled here, listening to the hubbub of talk, the clatter of crockery from the kitchen of the inn. Fitzraven finished his work and came over to his new employer.

"Would the Commander like to sample the night life in the Grand Corrida?"

"Not tonight," Retief said. "Let's go up to my quarters; I want to learn a little more about what to expect."

Retief's room, close under the rafters on the fourth floor of the inn, was small but adequate, with a roomy wardrobe and a wide bed. The contents of his saddlebags were already in place in the room.

Retief looked around. "Who gave you permission to open my saddlebags?"

Fitzraven flushed slightly, "I thought the Commander would wish to have them unpacked," he said stiffly.

"I looked at the job the other squires were doing on their horses," Retief said. "You were the only one who was doing a proper job of tending the animal. Why the special service?"

"I was trained by my father," Fitzraven said. "I serve only true knights, and I perform my duties honorably. If the Commander is dissatisfied…"

"How do you know I'm a true knight?"

"The Commander wears the uniform and weapons of one of the oldest Imperial Guards Battle Units, the Iron Dragon," Fitzraven said. "And the Commander rides a battle horse, true bred."

"How do you know I didn't steal them?"

Fitzraven grinned suddenly. "They fit the Commander too well."

Retief smiled. "All right, son, you'll do," he said. "Now brief me on the First Day. I don't want to miss anything. And you may employ the personal pronoun."

For an hour Fitzraven discussed the order of events for the elimination contests of the First Day of the Tournament of the Lily, the strategies that a clever contender could employ to husband his strength, the pitfalls into which the unwary might fall.

The tournament was the culmination of a year of smaller contests held throughout the equatorial chain of populated islands. The Northroyalans had substituted various forms of armed combat for the sports practiced on most worlds; a compensation for the lost empire, doubtless, a primitive harking-back to an earlier, more glorious day.

Out of a thousand First Day entrants, less than one in ten would come through to face the Second Day. Of course, the First Day events were less lethal than those to be encountered farther along in the three day tourney, Retief learned; there would be a few serious injuries in the course of the opening day, and those would be largely due to the clumsiness or ineptitude on the part of the entrants.

There were no formal entrance requirements, Fitzraven said, other than proof of minimum age and status in the Empire. Not all the entrants were natives of Northroyal; many came from distant worlds, long scattered descendants of the citizens of the shattered Lily Empire. But all competed for the same prizes; status in the Imperial peerage, the honors of the Field of the Emerald crown, and Imperial grants of land, wealth to the successful.

"Will you enter the First Day events, sir," Fitzraven asked, "or do you have a second or third day certification?"

"Neither," Retief said. "We'll sit on the sidelines and watch."

Fitzraven looked surprised. It had somehow not occurred to him that the old man was not to be a combatant. And it was too late to get seats.

"How..." Fitzraven began, after a pause.

"Don't worry," Retief said. "We'll have a place to sit."

Fitzraven fell silent, tilted his head to one side, listening. Loud voices, muffled by walls, the thump of heavy feet.

"Something is up," Fitzraven said. "Police." He looked at Retief.

"I wouldn't be surprised," Retief said, "if they were looking for me. Let's go find out."

"We need not meet them," the squire said. "There is another way..."

"Never mind," Retief said, "as well now as later." He winked at Fitzraven and turned to the door.

RETIEF STEPPED off the lift into the crowded common room, Fitzraven at his heels. Half a dozen men in dark blue tunics and tall shakos moved among the patrons, staring at faces. By the door Retief saw the thin-mouthed Ensign he had over-awed at the gate. The fellow saw him at the same moment and plucked at the sleeve of the nearest policeman, pointing.

The man dropped a hand to his belt, and at once the other policeman turned, followed his glance to Retief. They moved toward him with one accord. Retief stood waiting.

The first cop planted himself before Retief, looking him up and down. "Your papers!" he snapped.

Retief smiled easily. "I am a peer of the Lily and a Battle officer of the Imperial forces," he said. "On what pretext are you demanding papers of me, Captain?"

The cop raised his eyebrows.

"Let's say you are charged with unauthorized entry into the controlled area of the Grand Corrida, and with impersonating an Imperial officer," he said. "You didn't expect to get away with it, did you grandpa?" The fellow smiled sardonically.

"Under the provisions of the Code," Retief said, "the status of a peer may not be questioned, nor his actions interfered with except by Imperial Warrant. Let me see yours, Captain. And I suggest you assume a more courteous tone when addressing your superior officer." Retief's voice hardened to a whip crack with the last words.

The policeman stiffened, scowled. His hand dropped to the nightstick at his belt.

"None of your insolence, old man," he snarled. "Papers! Now!"

Retief's hand shot out, gripped the officer's hand over the stick. "Raise that stick," he said quietly," and I'll assuredly beat out your brains with it." He smiled calmly into the captain's bulging eyes. The captain was a strong man. He threw every ounce of his strength into the effort to bring up his arm, to pull free of the old man's grasp. The crowd of customers, the squad of police, stood silently, staring, uncertain of what was going on, Retief stood steady; the officer strained, reddened. The old man's arm was like cast steel.

"I see you are using your head, Captain," Retief said. "Your decision not to attempt to employ force against a peer was an intelligent one."

The cop understood. He was being offered an opportunity to save a little face. He relaxed slowly.

"Very well, uh, sir," he said stiffly, "I will assume you can establish your identity properly; kindly call at the commandant's office in the morning."

Retief released his hold and the officer hustled his men out, shoving the complaining Ensign ahead, Fitzraven caught Retief's eye and grinned.

"Empty pride is a blade with no hilt," he said. "A humble man would have yelled for help."

Retief turned to the barman. "Drinks for all," he called. A happy shout greeted this announcement. They had all enjoyed seeing the police outfaced.

"The cops don't seem to be popular here," the old man said.

Fitzraven sniffed. "A law-abiding subject parks illegally for five minutes, and they are on him like flies after dead meat; but let his car be stolen by lawless hoodlums—they are nowhere to be seen."

"That has a familiar sound," Retief said. He poured out a tumbler of vodka, looked at Fitzraven.

"Tomorrow," he said. "A big day."

A tall blonde young man near the door looked after him with bitter eyes.

"All right, old man," he muttered. "We'll see then."

CHAPTER THREE

The noise of the crowd came to Retief's ears as a muted rumble through the massive pile of the amphitheater above. A dim light filtered, from the low-ceilinged corridor into the cramped office of the assistant Master of the Games.

"If you know your charter," Retief said, "you will recall that a Battle Commander enjoys the right to observe the progress of the games from the official box, I claim that privilege."

"I know nothing of this," the cadaverous official replied impatiently. "You must obtain an order from the Master of the Games before I can listen to you." He turned to another flunkey, opened his mouth to speak. A hand seized him by the shoulder, lifted him bodily from his seat. The man's mouth remained open in shock.

Retief held the stricken man at arm's length, then drew him closer. His eyes blazed into the gaping eyes of the other. His face was white with fury.

"Little man," he said in a strange, harsh voice, "I go now with my groom to take my place in the official box. Read your Charter well before you interfere with me—and your Holy Book as well." He dropped the fellow with a crash, saw him slide under the desk. No one made a sound. Even Fitzraven looked pale. The force of the old man's rage had been like a lethal radiation crackling in the room.

The squire followed as Retief strode off down the corridor. He breathed deeply, wiping his forehead. This was some old man he had met this year, for sure!

Retief slowed, turning to wait for Fitzraven. He smiled ruefully. "I was rough on the old goat," he said. "But officious pipsqueaks sting me like deerflies."

They emerged from the gloom of the passage into a well-situated box, to the best seats in the first row. Retief stared at the white glare and roiled dust of the arena, the banked thousands of faces looming above, and a sky of palest blue with one tiny white cloud. The gladiators stood in little groups, waiting. A strange scene, Retief thought. A scene from dim antiquity, but real, complete with the odors of fear and excitement, the hot wind that ruffled his hair, the rumbling animal sound from the thousand throats of the many-headed monster. He wondered what it was they really wanted to see here today. A triumph of skill and courage, a reaffirmation of ancient virtues, the spectacle of men who laid life on the gaming table and played for a prize called glory—or was it merely blood and death they wanted?

It was strange that this archaic ritual of the blood tournament, combining the features of the Circus of Caesar, the joust of Medieval Terran Europe, the Olympic Games, a rodeo, and a six-day bicycle race should have come to hold such an important place in a modern culture, Retief thought. In its present form it was a much distorted version of the traditional Tournament of the Lily, through whose gauntlet the nobility of the old Empire had come. It had been a device of harsh enlightenment to insure and guarantee to every man, once each year, the opportunity to prove himself against others whom society called his betters. Through its discipline, the humblest farm lad could rise by degrees to the highest levels in the Empire. For the original Games had tested every facet of a man, from his raw courage to his finesse in strategy, from his depths of endurance under mortal stress to the quickness of his intellect, from his instinct for truth to his wilyness in eluding a complex trap of violence.

In the two centuries since the fall of the Empire, the Games had gradually become a tourist spectacle, a free-for-all, a celebration—with the added spice of danger for those who did not shrink back, and fat prizes to a few determined finalists. The Imperial Charter was still invoked at the opening of the Games, the old Code reaffirmed; but there were few who knew or cared what the Charter and Code actually said, what terms existed there. The popular mind left such details to the regents of the tourney. And in recent months, with the once sought-after tourists suddenly and inexplicably turned away, it seemed the Games were being perverted to a purpose even less admirable…

Well, thought Retief, perhaps I'll bring some of the fine print into play, before I'm done.

BUGLE BLASTS sounded beyond the high bronze gate. Then with a heavy clang it swung wide and a nervous official stepped out nodding jerkily to the front rank of today's contenders.

The column moved straight out across the field, came together with other columns to form a square before the Imperial box. High above, Retief saw banners fluttering, a splash of color from the uniforms of ranked honor guards. The Emperor himself was here briefly to open the Tournament.

Across the field the bugles rang out again; Retief recognized the *Call to Arms* and the *Imperial Salute*. Then an amplified voice began the ritual reading of the Terms of the Day.

"...by the clement dispensation of his Imperial Majesty, to be conducted under the convention of Fragonard, and there be none dissenting..." The voice droned on.

It finished at last, and referees moved to their positions. Retief looked at Fitzraven. "The excitement's about to begin."

Referees handed out heavy whips, gauntlets and face shields. The first event would be an unusual one.

Retief watched as the yellow-haired combatant just below the box drew on the heavy leather glove that covered and protected the left hand and forearm, accepted the fifteen-foot lash of braided oxhide. He flipped it tentatively, laying the length out along the ground and recalling it with an effortless turn of the wrist, the frayed tip snapping like a pistol shot. The thing was heavy, Retief noted, and clumsy; the leather had no life to it.

The box had filled now; no one bothered Retief and the squire. The noisy crowd laughed and chattered, called to acquaintances in the stands and on the field below.

A bugle blasted peremptorily nearby, and white-suited referees darted among the milling entrants, shaping them into groups of five, Retief watched the blonde youth, a tall frowning man, and three others of undistinguished appearance.

Fitzraven leaned toward him. "The cleverest will hang back and let the others eliminate each other," he said in a low voice, "so that his first encounter will be for the set."

Retief nodded. A man's task here was to win his way as high as possible; every stratagem was important. He saw the blonde fellow inconspicuously edge back as a hurrying referee paired off the other four, called to him to stand by, and led the others to rings marked off on the dusty turf. A whistle blew suddenly, and over the arena the roar of sound changed tone. The watching crowd leaned forward as the hundreds of keyed up gladiators laid on their lashes in frenzied effort. Whips cracked, men howled, feet shuffled; here the crowd laughed as some clumsy fellow sprawled, yelping; there they gasped in excitement as two surly brutes flogged each other in all-out offense.

Retief saw the tip of one man's whip curl around his opponent's ankle, snatch him abruptly off his feet. The other pair circled warily, rippling their lashes uncertainly. One backed over the line unnoticing and was led away expostulating, no blow having been struck.

The number on the field dwindled away to half within moments. Only a few dogged pairs, now bleeding from cuts, still contested the issue. A minute longer and the whistle blew as the last was settled.

The two survivors of the group below paired off now, and as the whistle blasted again, the tall fellow, still frowning, brought the other to the ground with a single sharp flick of the lash. Retief looked him over. This was a man to watch.

More whistles, and a field now almost cleared; only two men left out of each original five: the blond moved out into the circle, stared across at the other. Retief recognized him suddenly as the fellow who had challenged him outside the gate, over the spilled fruit. So he had followed through the arch.

The final whistle sounded and a hush fell over the watchers. Now the shuffle of feet could be heard clearly, the hissing breath of the weary fighters, the creak and slap of leather.

The blonde youth flipped his lash out lightly, saw it easily evaded, stepped aside from a sharp counter-blow. He feinted, reversed the direction of his cast, and caught the other high on the chest as he dodged aside. A welt showed instantly. He saw a lightning-fast riposte on the way, sprang back. The gauntlet came up barely in time. The lash wrapped around the gauntlet, and the young fellow seized the leather and hauled sharply. The other stumbled forward. The blond brought his whip across the fellow's back in a tremendous slamming blow that sent a great fragment of torn shirt flying. Somehow the man stayed on his feet, backed off, circled. His opponent followed up, laying down one whistling whip crack after another, trying to drive the other over the line. He had hurt the man with the cut across the back, and now was attempting to finish him easily.

He leaned away from a sluggish pass, and then Retief saw agony explode in his face as a vicious cut struck home. The blonde youth reeled in a drunken circle, out on his feet.

Slow to follow up, the enemy's lash crashed across the circle; the youth, steadying quickly, slipped under it, struck at the other's stomach. The leather cannoned against the man and sent the remainder of his shirt fluttering in a spatter of blood. With a surge of shoulder and wrist that made the muscles creak, the blonde reversed the stroke, brought the lash back in a vicious cut aimed at the same spot. It struck, smacking with a wet explosive crack. And he struck again, again, as the fellow tottered back, fell over the line.

The winner went limp suddenly, staring across at the man who lay in the dust, pale now, moving feebly for a moment, then slackly still. There was a great deal of blood, and more blood. Retief saw with sudden shock that the man was disemboweled. That boy, thought Retief, plays for keeps.

The next two events constituting the First Day trials were undistinguished exhibitions of a two-handed version of old American Indian wrestling and a brief bout of fencing with blunt-tipped weapons. Eighty men were certified for the Second Day before noon, and Retief and Fitzraven were back in the inn room a few minutes later. "Take some time off now while I catch up on my rest," Retief said. "Have some solid food ready when I wake." Then he retired for the night.

With his master breathing heavily in a profound sleep, the squire went down to the common room and found a table at the back, ordered a mug of strong ale, and sat alone, thinking.

This was a strange one he had met this year. He had seen at once that he was no idler from some high-pressure world, trying to lose himself in a fantasy of the old days. And no more was he a Northroyalan; there was a grim force in him, a time-engraved stamp of power that was alien to the neat well-ordered little world. And yet there was no doubt that there was more in him of the true Cavalier than in a Fragonard-born courtier. He was like some ancient warrior noble from the days of the greatness of the Empire. By the two heads, the old man was strange, and terrible in anger!

Fitzraven listened to the talk around him.

"I was just above," a blacksmith at the next table was saying. "He gutted the fellow with the lash! It was monstrous! I'm glad I'm not one of the fools who want to play at warrior. Imagine having your insides drawn out by a rope of dirty leather!"

"The games have to be tougher now," said another. "We've lain dormant here for two centuries, waiting for something to come—something to set us on our way again to power and wealth…"

"Thanks, I'd rather go on living quietly as a smith and enjoying a few of the simple pleasures—there was no glory in that fellow lying in the dirt with his belly torn open, you can be sure of that."

"There'll be more than torn bellies to think about, when we mount a battle fleet for Grimwold and Tania," said another.

"The Emperor has returned," snapped the war-like one. "Shall we hang back where he leads?"

The smith muttered. "His is a tortured genealogy, by my judgment. I myself trace my ancestry by three lines into the old Palace at Lily."

"So do we all. All the more reason we should support our Emperor."

"We live well here; we have no quarrel with other worlds. Why not leave the past to itself?"

"Our Emperor leads; we will follow. If you disapprove, enter the Lily Tournament next year and win a high place; then your advice will be respected."

"No thanks, I like my insides to stay on the inside."

Fitzraven thought of Retief. The old man had said that he held his rank in his own right, citing no genealogy. That was strange indeed. The Emperor had turned up only a year ago, presenting the Robe, the Ring, the Seal, the crown jewels, and the Imperial Book that traced his descent through five generations from the last reigning Emperor of the Old Empire.

How could it be that Retief held a commission in his own right, dated no more than thirty years ago? And the rank of Battle Commander. That was a special rank, Fitzraven remembered, a detached rank for a distinguished noble and officer of proven greatness, assigned to no one unit, but dictating his own activities.

Either Retief was a fraud…but Fitzraven pictured the old man, his chiseled features that time had not disguised, his soldier's bearing, his fantastic strength, his undoubtedly authentic equipage. Whatever the explanation, he was a true knight. That was enough.

CHAPTER FOUR

Retief awoke refreshed, and ravenous. A great rare steak and a giant tankard of autumn ale were ready on the table. He ate, ordered more and ate again. Then he stretched, shook himself, no trace of yesterday's fatigue remaining. His temper was better, too, he realized. He was getting too old to exhaust himself.

"It's getting late, Fitzraven," he said. "Let's be going."

They arrived at the arena and took their places in the official box in time to watch the first event, a cautious engagement with swords.

After four more events and three teams of determined but colorless competition, only a dozen men were left on the field awaiting the next event, including the tall blonde youth whom Retief had been watching since he had recognized him. He himself, he reflected, was the reason for the man's presence here; and he had acquitted himself well.

Retief saw a burly warrior carrying a two-handed sword paired off now against the blonde youth. The fellow grinned as he moved up to face the other.

This would be a little different, the agent thought watching; this fellow was dangerous. Yellow-hair moved in, his weapon held level across his chest. The big man lashed out suddenly with the great sword, and the other jumped back, then struck backhanded at his opponent's shoulder, nicked him lightly, sliding back barely in time to avoid a return swing. The still grinning man moved in, the blade chopping the air before him in a whistling figure eight. He pressed his man back, the blade never pausing.

There was no more room; the blonde fellow jumped sideways, dropping the point of his sword in time to intercept a vicious cut. He back-stepped; he couldn't let that happen again. The big man was very strong.

The blade was moving again now, the grin having faded a little. He'll have to keep away from him, keep circling, Retief thought. The big fellow's pattern is to push his man back to the edge, then pick him off as he tries to sidestep. He'll have to keep space between them.

The fair-haired man backed, watching for an opening. He jumped to the right, and as the other shifted to face him, leaped back to the left and catching the big man at the end of his reach to the other side, slashed him across the ribs and kept moving. The man roared, twisting around in vicious cuts at the figure that darted sideways, just out of range. Then the blond brought his claymore across in a low swing that struck solidly across the back of the other's legs, with a noise like a butcher separating ribs with a cleaver.

Like a marionette with his strings cut, the man folded to his knees, sprawled. The other man stepped back, as surgeons' men swarmed up to tend the fallen fighter. There were plenty of them available now; so far the casualties had been twice normal. On the other mounds in view, men were falling. The faint-hearted had been eliminated; the men who were still on their feet were determined, or desperate. There would be no more push-overs.

"Only about six left," Fitzraven called.

"This has been a rather unusual tournament so far," Retief said. "That young fellow with the light hair seems to be playing rough, forcing the pace."

"I have never seen such a business-like affair," Fitzraven said. "The weak-disposed have been frightened out, and the fighters cut down with record speed. At this rate there will be none left for the Third Day."

There was delay on the field, as referees and other officials hurried back and forth; then an announcement boomed out. The Second Day was officially concluded. The six survivors would be awarded Second Day certificates, and would be eligible for the Third and Last Day tomorrow.

Retief and Fitzraven left the box, made their way through the crowd back to the inn.

"See that Danger-by-Night is well fed and exercised," Retief said to the squire. "And check over all of my gear thoroughly. I wish to put on my best appearance tomorrow; it will doubtless be my last outing of the kind for some time."

Fitzraven hurried away to tend his chores, while Retief ascended to his room to pore over the contents of his dispatch case far into the night.

THE THIRD DAY had dawned gray and chill, and an icy wind whipped across the arena. The weather had not discouraged the crowd, however. The stands were packed and the overflow of people stood in the aisles, perched high on the back walls, crowding every available space. Banners flying from the imperial box indicated the presence of the royal party. This was the climactic day. The field, by contrast, was almost empty; two of the Second Day winners had not reentered for today's events, having apparently decided that they had had enough honor for one year. They would receive handsome prizes, and respectable titles; that was enough.

The four who had come to the arena today to stake their winning and their lives on their skill at arms would be worth watching Retief thought. There was the blonde young fellow, still unmarked; a great swarthy ruffian; a tall broad man of perhaps thirty; and a squat bowlegged fellow with enormous shoulders and long arms. They were here to win or die.

From the officials' box Retief and Fitzraven had an excellent view of the arena, where a large circle had been marked out. The officials seated nearby had given them cold glances as they entered, but no one had attempted to interfere. Apparently, they had accepted the situation. Possibly, Retief thought, they had actually studied the charter. He hoped they had studied it carefully. It would make things easier.

Announcements boomed, officials moved about, fanfares blasted, while Retief sat absorbed in thought. The scene reminded him of things he had long forgotten, days long gone, of his youth, when he had studied the martial skills, serving a long apprenticeship under his world's greatest masters. It had been his father's conviction that nothing so trained the eye and mind and body as fencing, judo, savete, and the disciplines of the arts of offense, and defense.

He had abandoned a priceless education when he had left his home to seek his fortune in the main stream of galactic culture, but it had stood him in good stead on more than one occasion. An agent of the Corps could not afford to let himself decline into physical helplessness, and Retief had maintained his skills as well as possible. He leaned forward now, adjusting his binoculars as the bugles rang out. Few in the crowd were better qualified than Retief to judge today's performance. It would be interesting to see how the champions handled themselves on the field.

The first event was about to begin, as the blonde warrior was paired off with the bow-legged man. The two had been issued slender foils, and now faced each other, blades crossed. A final whistle blew, and blade clashed on blade. The squat man was fast on his feet, bouncing around in a semi-circle before his taller antagonist, probing his defense with great energy. The blonde man backed away slowly, fending off the rain of blows with slight motions of his foil. He jumped back suddenly, and Retief saw a red spot grow on his thigh. The ape-like fellow was more dangerous than he had appeared.

Now the blonde man launched his attack, beating aside the weapon of the other and striking in for the throat, only to have his point deflected at the last instant. The short man backed now, giving ground reluctantly. Suddenly he dropped into a grotesque crouch, and lunged under the other's defense in a desperate try for a quick kill. It was a mistake; the taller man whirled aside, and his blade flicked delicately once. The bowlegged man slid out flat on his face.

"What happened?" Fitzraven said, puzzled. "I didn't see the stroke that nailed him."

"It was very pretty," Retief said thoughtfully, lowering the glasses. "Under the fifth rib and into the heart."

Now the big dark man and the tall broad fellow took their places. The bugles and whistles sounded, and the two launched a furious exchange, first one and then the other forcing his enemy back before losing ground in turn. The crowd roared its approval as the two stamped and thrust, parried and lunged.

"They can't keep up this pace forever," Fitzraven said. "They'll have to slow down."

"They're both good," Retief said. "And evenly matched."

Now the swarthy fellow leaped back, switched the foil to his left hand, then moved quickly in to the attack. Thrown off his pace, the other man faltered, let the blade nick him on the chest, again in the arm. Desperate, he back-pedaled, fighting defensively now. The dark man followed up his advantage, pressing savagely, and a moment later Retief saw a foot of bright steel projecting startlingly from the tall man's back. He took two steps, then folded, as the foil was wrenched from the dark man's hand.

Wave upon wave of sound rolled across the packed stands. Never had they seen such an exhibition as this! It was like the legendary battle of the heroes of the Empire, the fighters who had carried the Lily banner half across the galaxy.

"I'm afraid that's all," Fitzraven said. "These two can elect either to share the victory of the Tourney now, or to contend for sole honors, and in the history of the Tournament on Northroyal, there have never been fewer than three to share the day."

"It looks as though this is going to be the first time, then," Retief said. "They're getting ready to square off."

Below on the field, a mass of officials surrounded the dark man and the fair one, while the crowd outdid itself. Then a bugle sounded in an elaborate salute.

"That's it," Fitzraven said excitedly. "Heroes' Salute. They're going to do it."

"You don't know how glad I am to hear that," Retief said.

"What will the weapon be?" the squire wondered aloud.

"My guess is, something less deadly than the foil," Retief replied.

Moments later the announcement came. The two champions of the day would settle the issue with bare hands. This, thought Retief, would be something to see.

The fanfares and whistles rang out again, and the two men moved cautiously together. The dark man swung an open-handed blow, which smacked harmlessly against the other's shoulder. An instant later the blonde youth feinted a kick and instead drove a hard left to the dark man's chin, staggering him. He followed up, smashing two blows to the stomach, then another to the head. The dark man moved back, suddenly reached for the blonde man's wrist as he missed a jab, whirled, and attempted to throw his opponent. The blonde man slipped aside, and locked his right arm over the dark man's head, seizing his own right wrist with his left hand. The dark man twisted, fell heavily on the other man, reaching for a headlock of his own.

The two rolled in the dust, then broke apart and were on their feet again. The dark man moved in, swung an openhanded slap which popped loudly against the blonde man's face. It was a device, Retief saw, to enrage the man, dull the edge of his skill.

The blonde man refused to be rattled, however; he landed blows against the dark man's head, evaded another attempt to grapple. It was plain that he preferred to avoid the other's bear-like embrace. He boxed carefully, giving ground, landing a blow as the opportunity offered. The dark man followed doggedly, seemingly unaffected by the pounding. Suddenly he leaped, took two smashing blows full in the face, and crashed against the blonde man, knocking him to the ground. There was a flying blur of flailing arms and legs as the two rolled across the turf, and as they came to rest, Retief saw that the dark man had gotten his break. Kneeling behind the other, he held him in a rigid stranglehold, his back and shoulder muscles bulging with the effort of holding his powerful adversary immobilized.

"It's all over," Fitzraven said tensely.

"Maybe not," Retief replied. "Not if he plays it right, and doesn't panic."

The blonde man strained at the arm locked at his throat, twisting it fruitlessly. Instinct drove him to tear at the throttling grip, throw off the smothering weight. But the dark man's grip was solid, his position unshakable. Then the blond stopped struggling abruptly and the two seemed as still as an image in stone. The crowd fell silent, fascinated.

"He's given up," Fitzraven said.

"No; watch," Retief said. "He's starting to use his head."

The blonde man's arms reached up now, his hands moving over the other's head, seeking a grip. The dark man pulled his head in, pressing against his victim's back, trying to elude his grip. Then the hands found a hold, and the blonde man bent suddenly forward, heaving with a tremendous surge. The dark man came up, flipped high, his grip slipping. The blond rose as the other went over his head, shifted his grip in midair, and as the dark man fell heavily in front of him, the snap of the spine could be heard loud in the stillness. The battle was over, and the blonde victor rose to his feet amid a roar of applause.

Retief turned to Fitzraven. "Time for us to be going, Fitz," he said. The squire jumped up. "As you command, sir; but the ceremony is quite interesting…"

"Never mind that; let's go." Retief moved off, Fitzraven following, puzzled.

Retief descended the steps inside the stands, turned and started down the corridor.

"This way, sir," Fitzraven called. "That leads to the arena."

"I know it," Retief said. "That's where I'm headed."

Fitzraven hurried up alongside. What was the old man going to do now? "Sir," he said, "no one may enter the arena until the tourney has been closed, except the gladiators and the officials. I know this to be an unbreakable law."

"That's right, Fitz," Retief said. "You'll have to stop at the grooms' enclosure."

"But you, sir," Fitzraven gasped.

"Everything's under control," Retief said. "I'm going to challenge the Champion."

CHAPTER FIVE

In the Imperial box, the Emperor Rolan leaned forward, fixing his binoculars on a group of figures at the officials' gate. There seemed to be some sort of disturbance there. This was a piece of damned impudence, just as the moment had arrived for the Imperial presentation of the Honors of the Day. The Emperor turned to an aide.

"What the devil's going on down there?" he snapped.

The courtier murmured into a communicator, listened.

"A madman, Imperial Majesty," he said smoothly. "He wished to challenge the champion."

"A drunk, more likely," Rolan said sharply. "Let him be removed at once. And tell the Master of the Games to get on with the ceremony!"

The Emperor turned to the slim dark girl at his side.

"Have you found the Games entertaining, Monica?"

"Yes, sire," she replied unemotionally.

"Don't call me that, Monica," he said testily. "Between us there is no need of formalities."

"Yes, Uncle," the girl said.

"Damn it, that's worse," he said. "To you I am simply Rolan." He placed his hand firmly on her silken knee. "And now if they'll get on with this tedious ceremony, I should like to be on the way. I'm looking forward with great pleasure to showing you my estates at Snowdahl."

The Emperor drummed his fingers, stared down at the field, raised the glasses only to see the commotion again.

"Get that fool off the field," he shouted, dropping the glasses. "Am I to wait while they haggle with this idiot? It's insufferable…"

Courtiers scurried, while Rolan glared down from his seat.

Below, Retief faced a cluster of irate referees. One, who had attempted to haul Retief bodily backward, was slumped on a bench, attended by two surgeons.

"I claim the right to challenge, under the Charter," Retief repeated. "Nobody here will be so foolish, I hope, as to attempt to deprive me of that right, now that I have reminded you of the justice of my demand."

From the control cage directly below the Emperor's high box, a tall seam-faced man in black breeches and jacket emerged, followed by two armed men. The officials darted ahead, stringing out between the two, calling out. Behind Retief, on the other side of the barrier, Fitzraven watched anxiously. The old man was full of surprises, and had a way of getting what he wanted; but even if he had the right to challenge the Champion of the Games, what purpose could he have in doing so? He was as strong as a bull, but no man his age could be a match for the youthful power of the blonde fighter, Fitzraven was worried; he was fond of this old warrior. He would hate to see him locked behind the steel walls of Fragonard Keep for thus disturbing the order of the Lily Tournament. He moved closer to the barrier, watching.

The tall man in black strode through the chattering officials, stopped before Retief, motioned his two guards forward.

He made a dismissing motion toward Retief. "Take him off the field," he said brusquely. The guards stepped up, laid hands on Retief's arms. He let them get a grip, then suddenly stepped back and brought his arms together. The two men cracked heads, stumbled back. Retief looked at the black-clad man.

"If you are the Master of the Games," he said clearly, "you are well aware that a decorated Battle Officer has the right of challenge, under the Imperial Charter, I invoke that prerogative now, to enter the lists against the man who holds the field."

"Get out, you fool," the official hissed, white with fury. "The Emperor himself has commanded…"

"Not even the Emperor can override the Charter, which predates his authority by four hundred years," Retief said coldly. "Now do your duty."

"There'll be no more babble of duties and citing of technicalities while the Emperor waits," the official snapped. He turned to one of the two guards who hung back now, eyeing Retief. "You have a pistol; draw it. If I give the command, shoot him between the eyes."

Retief reached up and adjusted a tiny stud set in the stiff collar of his tunic. He tapped his finger lightly against the cloth. The sound boomed across the arena. A command microphone of the type authorized a Battle Commander was a very efficient device.

"I have claimed the right to challenge the champion," he said slowly. The words rolled out like thunder. "This right is guaranteed under the Charter to any Imperial Battle officer who wears the Silver Star."

The Master of the Games stared at him aghast. This was getting out of control. Where the devil had the old man gotten a microphone and a P. A. system? The crowd was roaring now like a gigantic surf. This was something new!

Far above in the Imperial box the tall gray-eyed man was rising, turning toward the exit. "The effrontery," he said in a voice choked with rage. "That I should sit awaiting the pleasure..."

The girl at his side hesitated, hearing the amplified voice booming across the arena.

"Wait...Rolan," she said. "Something is happening..."

The man looked back. "A trifle late," he snapped.

"One of the contestants is disputing something," she said. "There was an announcement—something about an Imperial officer challenging the champion."

The Emperor Rolan turned to an aide hovering nearby.

"What is this nonsense?"

The courtier bowed. "It is merely a technicality, Majesty. A formality lingering on from earlier times."

"Be specific," the Emperor snapped.

The aide lost some of his aplomb. "Why, it means, ah, that an officer of the Imperial forces holding a battle commission and certain high decorations may enter the lists at any point, without other qualifying conditions. A provision never invoked under modern..."

The Emperor turned to the girl. "It appears that someone seeks to turn the entire performance into a farcical affair, at my expense," he said bitterly. "We shall see just how far..."

"I call on you, Rolan," Retief's voice boomed, "to enforce the Code."

"What impertinence is this?" Rolan growled. "Who is the fool at the microphone?"

The aide spoke into his communicator, listened.

"An old man from the crowd, sire. He wears the insignia of a Battle-Commander, and a number of decorations, including the Silver Star. According to the Archivist, he has the legal right to challenge."

"I won't have it," Rolan snapped. "A fine reflection on me that would be. Have them take the fellow away; he's doubtless crazed," He left the box, followed by his entourage.

"Rolan," the girl said, "wasn't that the way the Tourneys were, back in the days of the Empire?"

"These are the days of the Empire, Monica. And I am not interested in what used to be done. This is today. Am I to present the spectacle of a doddering old fool being hacked to bits, in my name? I don't want the timid to be shocked by butchery. It might have unfortunate results for my propaganda program. I'm currently emphasizing the glorious aspects of the coming war, not the sordid ones. There has already been too much bloodshed today; an inauspicious omen for my expansion plan."

ON THE field below, the Master of the Games stepped closer to Retief. He felt the cold eyes of the Emperor himself boring into his back. This old devil could bring about his ruin…

"I know all about you," he snarled, "I've checked on you, since you forced your way into an official area; I interviewed two officers…you overawed them with glib talk and this threadbare finery you've decked yourself in. Now you attempt to ride rough-shod over me. Well, I'm not so easily thrust aside. If you resist arrest any further, I'll have you shot where you stand!"

Retief drew his sword.

"In the name of the Code you are sworn to serve," he said, his voice ringing across the arena, "I will defend my position." He reached up and flipped the stud at his throat to full pick-up.

"To the Pit with your infernal Code!" bellowed the Master, and blanched in horror as his words boomed sharp and clear across the field to the ears of a hundred thousand people. He stared around, then whirled back to Retief. "Fire," he screamed.

A pistol cracked, and the guard spun, dropped. Fitzraven held the tiny power gun leveled across the barrier at the other guard. "What next, sir?" he asked brightly.

The sound of the shot, amplified, smashed deafeningly across the arena, followed by a mob roar of excitement, bewilderment, shock. The group around Retief stood frozen, staring at the dead man. The Master of the Games made a croaking sound, eyes bulging. The remaining guard cast a glance at the pistol, then turned and ran.

There were calls from across the field; then a troop of brown-uniformed men emerged from an entry, trotted toward the group. The officer at their head carried a rapid fire shock gun in his hand. He waved his squad to a halt as he reached the fringe of the group. He stared at Retief's drab uniform, glanced at the corpse. Retief saw that the officer was young, determined looking, wearing the simple insignia of a Battle Ensign.

The Master of the Games found his voice. "Arrest this villain!" he screeched, pointing at Retief. "Shoot the murderer!"

The ensign drew himself to attention, saluted crisply.

"Your orders, sir," he said.

"I've told you!" the Master howled. "Seize this malefactor!"

The ensign turned to the black-clad official. "Silence, sir, or I shall be forced to remove you," he said sharply. He looked at Retief, "I await the Commander's orders."

Retief smiled, returned the young officer's salute with a wave of his sword, then sheathed it. "I'm glad to see a little sense displayed here, at last, Battle-Ensign," he said, "I was beginning to fear I'd fallen among Concordiatists."

The outraged Master began an harangue that was abruptly silenced by two riot police. He was led away, protesting. The other officials disappeared like a morning mist, carrying the dead guard.

"I've issued my challenge, Ensign," Retief said. "I wish it to be conveyed to the champion-apparent at once." He smiled. "And I'd like you to keep your men around to see that nothing interferes with the orderly progress of the Tourney in accordance with the Charter in its original form."

The ensign's eyes sparkled. Now here was a battle-officer who sounded like a fighting man; not a windbag like the commandant of the Household Regiment from whom the ensign took his orders. He didn't know where the old man came from, but any battle-officer outranked any civilian or flabby barracks-soldier, and this was a Battle Commander, a general officer, and of the Dragon Corps!

Minutes later, a chastened Master of the Games announced that a challenge had been issued. It was the privilege of the champion to accept, or to refuse the challenge if he wished. In the latter event, the challenge would automatically be met the following year.

"I don't know what your boys said to the man," Retief remarked, as he walked out to the combat circle, the ensign at his left side and slightly to the rear, "but they seem to have him educated quickly."

"They can be very persuasive, sir," the young officer replied.

They reached the circle, stood waiting. Now, thought Retief, I've got myself in the position I've been working toward. The question now is whether I'm still man enough to put it over.

He looked up at the massed stands, listening to the mighty roar of the crowd. There would be no easy out for him now. Of course, the new champion might refuse to fight; he had every right to do so, feeling he had earned his year's rest and enjoyment of his winnings. But that would be a defeat for Retief as final as death on the dusty ground of the arena. He had come this far by bluff, threat, and surprise. He would never come this close again.

It was luck that he had clashed with this young man outside the gate, challenged him to enter the lists. That might give the challenge the personal quality that would elicit an angry acceptance.

CHAPTER SIX

THE CHAMPION was walking toward Retief now, surrounded by referees. He stared at the old man, eyes narrowed, Retief returned the look calmly.

"Is this dodderer the challenger?" the blonde youth asked scathingly. "It seems to me I have met his large mouth before?"

"Never mind my mouth, merchant," Retief said loudly. "It is not talk I offer you, but the bite of steel."

The yellow-haired man reddened, then laughed shortly. "Small glory I'd win out of skewering you, old graybeard."

"You'd get even less out of showing your heels," Retief said.

"You will not provoke me into satisfying your perverted ambition to die here," the other retorted.

"It's interesting to note," Retief said, "how a peasant peddler wags his tongue to avoid a fight. Such rabble should not be permitted on honorable ground." He studied the other's face to judge how this line of taunting was going on. It was distasteful to have to embarrass the young fellow; he seemed a decent sort. But he had to enrage him to the point that he would discard his wisdom and throw his new-won prize on the table for yet another cast of the dice. And his sore point seemed to be mention of commerce.

"Back to your cabbages, then, fellow," Retief said harshly, "before I whip you there with the flat of my sword."

The young fellow looked at him, studying him. His face was grim. "All right," he said quietly. "I'll meet you in the circle."

Another point gained, Retief thought, as he moved to his position at the edge of the circle. Now, if I can get him to agree to fight on horseback...

He turned to a referee. "I wish to suggest that this contest be conducted on horseback—if the peddler owns a horse and is not afraid."

The point was discussed between the referee and the champion's attendants, with many glances at Retief, and much waving of arms. The official returned. "The champion agrees to meet you by day or by night, in heat or cold, on foot or on horseback."

"Good," said Retief. "Tell my groom to bring out my mount."

It was no idle impulse that prompted this move. Retief had no illusions as to what it would take to win a victory over the champion. He knew that his legs, while good enough for most of the business of daily life, were his weakest point. They were no longer the nimble tireless limbs that had once carried him up to meet the outlaw Mal de Di alone in Bifrost Pass. Nine hours later he had brought the bandit's two hundred and ten pound body down into the village on his back, his own arm broken. He had been a mere boy then, younger than this man he was now to meet. He had taken up Mal de Di's standing challenge to any unarmed man who would come alone to the high pass, to prove that he was not too young to play a man's part. Perhaps now he was trying to prove he was not too old...

An official approached leading Danger-by-Night. It took an expert to appreciate the true worth of the great gaunt animal, Retief knew. To the uninitiated eye, he presented a sorry appearance, but Retief would rather have had this mount with the imperial brand on his side, than a paddock full of show horses.

A fat white charger was led out to the blonde champion. It looked like a strong animal, Retief thought, but slow. His chances were looking better, things were going well.

A ringing blast of massed trumpets cut through the clamor of the crowd. Retief mounted, watching his opponent. A referee came to his side, handed up a heavy club, studded with long projecting spikes. "Your weapon, sir," he said.

Retief took the thing. It was massive, clumsy; he had never before handled such a weapon. He knew no subtleties of technique with this primitive bludgeon. The blonde youth had surprised him, he admitted to himself, smiling slightly. As the challenged party, he had the choice of weapons, of course. He had picked an unusual one.

Retief glanced across at Fitzraven, standing behind the inner barrier, jaw set, a grim expression on his face. That boy, thought Retief, doesn't have much confidence in my old bones holding out.

The whistle blew. Retief moved toward the other man at a trot, the club level at his side. He had decided to handle it like a short sword, so long as that seemed practical. He would have to learn by experience.

The white horse cantered past him swerving, and the blond fellow whirled his club at Retief's head. Automatically, Retief raised his club, fended off the blow, cut at the other's back, missed. This thing is too short, Retief thought, whirling his horse. I've got to get in closer. He charged at the champion as the white horse was still in mid-turn, slammed a heavy blow against his upraised club, rocking the boy; then he was past, turning again. He caught the white horse shorter this time, barely into his turn, and aimed a swing at the man who first twisted to face him, then spurred, leaped away. Retief pursued him, yelping loudly. Get him rattled, he thought. Get him good and mad!

The champion veered suddenly, veered again, then reared his horse high, whirling, to bring both forefeet down in a chopping attack. Retief reined in, and Danger-by-Night sidestepped disdainfully, as the heavy horse crashed down facing him.

That was a pretty maneuver, Retief thought; but slow, too slow.

His club swung in an overhand cut; the white horse tossed his head suddenly, and the club smashed down across the animal's skull. With a shuddering exhalation, the beast collapsed, and the blonde man sprang clear.

Retief reined back, dismayed. He hadn't wanted to kill the animal. He had the right, now, to ride the man down from the safety of the saddle. When gladiators met in mortal combat, there were no rules except those a man made for himself. If he dismounted, met his opponent on equal terms, the advantage his horse had given him would be lost. He looked at the man standing now, facing him, waiting, blood on his face from the fall. He thought of the job he had set himself, the plan that hinged on his victory here. He reminded himself that he was old, too old to meet youth on equal terms; but even as he did so, he was reining the lean battle stallion back, swinging down from the saddle. There were some things a man had to do, whether logic was served or not. He couldn't club the man down like a mad dog from the saddle.

There was a strange expression on the champion's face. He sketched a salute with the club he held. "All honor to you, old man," he said. "Now I will kill you." He moved in confidently.

Retief stood his ground, raising his club to deflect a blow, shifting an instant ahead of the pattern of the blonde man's assault. There was a hot exchange as the younger man pressed him, took a glancing blow on the temple, stepped back breathing heavily. This wasn't going as he had planned. The old man stood like a wall of stone, not giving an inch; and when their weapons met, it was like flailing at a granite boulder. The young fellow's shoulder ached from the shock. He moved sideways, circling cautiously.

Retief moved to face him. It was risky business, standing up to the attack, but his legs were not up to any fancy footwork. He had no desire to show his opponent how stiff his movements were, or to tire himself with skipping about. His arms were still as good as any man's, or better. They would have to carry the battle.

The blonde jumped in, swung a vicious cut; Retief leaned back, hit out in a one-handed blow, felt the club smack solidly against the other's jaw. He moved now, followed up, landed again on the shoulder. The younger man backed, shaking his head. Retief stopped, waited. It was too bad he couldn't follow up his advantage, but he couldn't chase the fellow all over the arena. He had to save his energy for an emergency. He lowered his club, leaned on it. The crowd noises waxed and waned, unnoticed. The sun beat down in unshielded whiteness, and fitful wind moved dust across the field.

"Come back, peddler," he called. "I want you to sample more of my wares." If he could keep the man angry, he would be careless; and Retief needed the advantage.

The yellow-haired man charged suddenly, whirling the club. Retief raised his, felt the shock of the other's weapon against his. He whirled as the blonde darted around him, shifted the club to his left hand in time to ward off a wild swing. Then the fingers of his left hand exploded in fiery agony, and the club flew from his grasp. His head whirled, vision darkening, at the pain from his smashed fingers. He tottered, kept his feet, managed to blink away the faintness, to stare at this hand. Two fingers were missing, pulped, unrecognizable. He had lost his weapon; he was helpless now before the assault of the other.

His head hummed harshly, and his breath came like hot sand across an open wound. He could feel a tremor start and stop in his leg, and his whole left arm felt as though it had been stripped of flesh in a shredding machine. He had not thought it would be as bad as this. His ego, he realized, hadn't aged gracefully.

Now is the hour, old man, he thought. There's no help for you to call on, no easy way out. You'll have to look within yourself for some hidden reserve of strength and endurance and will; and you must think well now, wisely, with a keen eye and a quick hand, or lose your venture. With a moment stiffened by the racking pain-shock, he drew his ceremonial dagger, a jewel-encrusted blade ten inches long. At the least he would die with a weapon in his hand and his face to the enemy.

The blonde youth moved closer, tossed the club aside.

"Shall a peddler be less capable of the *beau geste* than the arrogant knight?" He laughed, drawing a knife from his belt. "Is your head clear, old man?" he asked. "Are you ready?"

"A gesture…you can…ill afford," Retief managed. Even breathing hurt. His nerves were shrieking their message of shock at the crushing of living flesh and bone. His forehead was pale, wet with cold sweat.

The young fellow closed, struck out, and Retief evaded the point by an inch, stepped back. His body couldn't stand pain as once it had, he was realizing. He had grown soft, sensitive. For too many years he had been a Diplomat, an operator by manipulation, by subtlety and finesse. Now, when it was man to man, brute strength against brute strength, he was failing.

But he had known when he started that strength was not enough, not without agility; it was subtlety he should be relying on now, his skill at trickery, his devious wit.

Retief caught a glimpse of staring faces at the edge of the field, heard for a moment the mob roar, and then he was again wholly concentrated on the business at hand.

He breathed deeply, struggling for clear-headedness. He had to inveigle the boy into a contest in which he stood a chance. If he could put him on his mettle, make him give up his advantage of tireless energy, quickness…

"Are you an honest peddler, or a dancing master," Retief managed to growl. "Stand and meet me face to face."

The blonde man said nothing, feinting rapidly, then striking out. Retief was ready and nicked the other's wrist.

"Gutter fighting is one thing," Retief said. "But you are afraid to face the old man's steel, right arm against right arm." If he went for that, Retief thought, he was even younger than he looked.

"I have heard of the practice." the blonde man said, striking at Retief, moving aside from a return cut. "It was devised for old men who did not wish to be made ridiculous by more agile men. I understand that you think you can hoodwink me, but I can beat you at your own game…"

"My point awaits your pleasure," Retief said.

The younger man moved closer, knife held before him. Just a little closer, Retief thought. Just a little closer.

The blonde man's eyes were on Retief's. Without warning, Retief dropped his knife and in a lightning motion caught the other's wrist.

"Now struggle, little fish," he said. "I have you fast."

The two men stood chest to chest, staring into each other's eyes, Retief's breath came hard, his heart pounded almost painfully. His left arm was a great pulsating weight of pain. Sweat ran down his dusty face into his eyes. But his grip was locked solidly. The blonde youth strained in vain.

With a twist of his wrist Retief turned the blade, then forced the youth's arm up. The fellow struggled to prevent it, throwing all his weight into his effort, fruitlessly. Retief smiled.

"I won't kill you," he said, "but I will have to break your arm. That way you cannot be expected to continue the fight."

"I want no favors from you, old man," the youth panted.

"You won't consider this a favor until the bones knit," Retief said. "Consider this a fair return for my hand."

He pushed the arm up, then suddenly turned it back, levered the upper arm over his forearm, and yanked the tortured member down behind the blonde man's back.

The bones snapped audibly, and the white-faced youth gasped, staggered as Retief released him.

There were minutes of confusion as referees rushed in, announcements rang out, medics hovered, and the crowd roared its satisfaction, after the fickle nature of crowds.

They were satisfied.

An official pushed through to Retief. He wore the vivid colors of the Review regiment. Retief reached up and set the control on the command mike.

"I have the honor to advise you, sir, that you have won the field, and the honors of the day." He paused, startled at the booming echoes, then went on. The bystanders watched curiously, as Retief tried to hold his concentration on the man, to stand easily, while blackness threatened to move in over him. The pain from the crushed hand swelled and focused, then faded, then came again. The great dry lungfulls of air he drew in failed to dispel the sensation of suffocation. He struggled to understand the words that seemed to echo from a great distance.

"And now in the name of the Emperor, for crimes against the peace and order of the Empire, I place you under arrest for trial before the High Court at Fragonard."

Retief drew a deep breath, gathered his thoughts to speak.

"Nothing," he said, "could possibly please me more."

CHAPTER SEVEN

The room was vast and ornate, and packed with dignitaries, high officials, peers of the Lily. Here in the great chamber known as the Blue Vault, the High Court sat in silent ranks, waiting.

The charges had been read, the evidence presented. The prisoner, impersonating a peer of the Lily and an officer of an ancient and honored Corps, had flaunted the law of Northroyal and the authority of the Emperor, capping his audacity with murder, done by the hand of his servant sworn. Had the prisoner anything to say?

Retief, alone in the prisoner's box in the center of the room, his arm heavily bandaged and deadened with dope, faced the court. This would be the moment when all his preparations would be put to the ultimate test. He had laid long plans toward this hour. The archives of the Corps were beyond comparison in the galaxy, and he had spent weeks there, absorbing every detail of the fact that had been recorded on the world of Northroyal, and on the Old Empire that had preceded it. And to the lore of the archives, he had added facts known to himself, data from his own wide experience. But would those tenuous threads of tradition, hearsay, rumor, and archaic record hold true now? That was the gamble on which his mission was staked. The rabbits had better be in the hat.

He looked at the dignitaries arrayed before him. It had been a devious route, but so far he had succeeded; he had before him the highest officials of the world, the High

Justices, the Imperial Archivist, the official keepers of the Charter and the Code, and of the protocols and rituals of the tradition on which this society was based. He had risked everything on his assault on the sacred stasis of the Tournament, but how else could he have gained the ears of this select audience, with all Northroyal tuned in to hear the end of the drama that a hundred thousand had watched build to its shattering climax?

Now it was his turn to speak. It had better be good.

"Peers of the realm," Retief said, speaking clearly and slowly, "the basis of the charges laid against me is the assumption that I have falsified my identity. Throughout, I have done no more than exercise the traditional rights of a general officer and of a Lilyan peer, and, as befits a Cavalier, I have resisted all attempts to deprive me of those honored prerogatives. While it is regrettable that the low echelon of officials appears to be ignorant of the status of a Lilyan Battle Commander, it is my confident assumption that here, before the ranking nobles of the Northroyalan peerage, the justice of my position will be recognized."

As Retief paused, a dour graybeard spoke up from the Justices' bench.

"Your claims are incoherent to this court. You are known to none of us; and if by chance you claim descent from some renegade who deserted his fellow cavaliers at the time of the Exile, you will find scant honor among honest men here. From this, it is obvious that you delude yourself in imagining that you can foist your masquerade on this court successfully."

"I am not native to Northroyal," Retief said, "nor do I claim to be. Nor am I a descendant of renegades. Are you gentlemen not overlooking the fact that there was one ship that did not accompany the cavaliers into exile, but escaped

Concordiat surveillance and retired to rally further opposition to the invasion?"

There was a flurry of muttered comment, the putting together of heads, and shuffling of papers. The High Justice spoke.

"This would appear to be a reference to the vessel bearing the person of the Emperor Roquelle and his personal suite..."

"That is correct," Retief said.

"You stray farther than ever from the credible," a justice snapped. "The entire royal household accompanied the Emperor Rolan on the happy occasion of his rejoining his subjects here at Northroyal a year ago."

"About that event, I will have more to say later," Retief said coolly. "For the moment, suffice it to say that I am a legitimate descendant..."

"It does indeed NOT suffice to say!" barked the High Justice. "Do you intend to instruct this court as to what evidence will be acceptable'?"

"A figure of speech, Milord," Retief said, "I am quite able to prove my statement."

"Very well," said the High Justice. "Let us see your proof, though I confess I cannot conceive of a satisfactory one."

Retief reached down, unsnapped the flat despatch case at his belt, and drew out a document.

"This is my proof of my bona fides," he said, "I present it in evidence that I have committed no fraud. I am sure that you will recognize an authentic commission-in-patent of the Emperor Roquelle. Please note that the seals are unbroken." He passed the paper over.

A page took the heavy paper, looped with faded red ribbon and plastered with saucer-sized seals, trotted over to the Justices' bench and handed it up to the High Justice. He took it, gazed at it, turning it over, then broke the crumbling seals. The nearby Justices leaned over to see this strange exhibit. It was a heavily embossed document of the Old Empire type, setting forth genealogy and honors, and signed in sprawling letters with the name of an emperor two centuries dead, sealed with his tarnished golden seal. The Justices stared in amazement. The document was worth a fortune.

"I ask that the lowermost paragraph be read aloud," Retief said. "The amendment of thirty years ago."

The High Justice hesitated, then waved a page to him, handed down the document. "Read the lowermost para-graph aloud," he said.

The page read in a clear, well-trained voice,

"KNOW ALL MEN BY THESE PRESENTS THAT WHEREAS: THIS OUR LOYAL SUBJECT AND PEER OF THE IMPERIAL LILY JAME JARL FREELORD OF THE RETIEF; OFFICER IMPERIAL OF THE GUARD; OFFICER OF BATTLE; HEREDITARY LEGIONNAIRE OF HONOR; CAVALIER OF THE LILY; DEFENDER OF SALIENT WEST; BY IMPERIAL GRACE OFFICER OF THE SILVER STAR; HAS BY HIS GALLANTRY FIDELITY AND SKILL BROUGHT HONOR TO THE IMPERIAL LILY:

AND WHEREAS WE PLACE SPECIAL CONFIDENCE AND ESTEEM IN THIS SUBJECT AND PEER: WE DO THEREFORE APPOINT AND COMMAND THAT HE SHALL FORTHWITH ASSUME AND HENCEFORTH BEAR THE HONORABLE RANK OF BATTLE COMMANDER:

AND THAT HE SHALL BEAR THE OBLIGATIONS AND ENJOY THE PRIVILEGES APPERTAINING THEREUNTO: AS SHALL HIS HEIRS FOREVER."

There was a silence in the chamber as the page finished reading. All eyes turned to Retief, who stood in the box, strange expression on his face.

The page handed the paper back up to the High Justice, who resumed his perusal.

"I ask that my retinal patterns now be examined, and matched to those coded on the amendment," Retief said. The High Justice beckoned to a Messenger, and the court waited a restless five minutes until the arrival of an expert who quickly made the necessary check. He went to the Justice's bench, handed up a report form, and left the court room. The magistrate glanced at the form, turned again to the document. Below Roquelle's seal were a number of amendments, each in turn signed and sealed. The justices spelled out the unfamiliar names.

"Where did you get this?" the High Justice demanded uncertainly.

"It has been the property of my family for nine generations," Retief replied.

Heads nodded over the document, gray beards wagged.

"How is it," asked a Justice, "that you offer in evidence a document bearing amendments validated by signatures and seals completely unknown to us? In order to impress this court, such a warrant might well bear the names of actual former emperors, rather than of fictitious ones. I note the lowermost amendment, purporting to be a certification of high military rank dated only thirty years ago is signed 'Ronare.' "

"I was at that time attached to the Imperial Suite-in-Exile," Retief said. "I commanded the forces of the Emperor Ronare."

The High Justice and a number of other members of the court snorted openly.

"This impertinence will not further your case," the old magistrate said sharply. "Ronare, indeed. You cite a non-existent authority. At the alleged time of issue of this warrant, the father of our present monarch held the Imperial fief at Trallend."

"At the time of the issue of this document," Retief said in ringing tones, "the father of your present ruler held the bridle when the Emperor mounted!"

An uproar broke out from all sides. The Master-at-arms pounded in vain for silence. At length a measure of order was restored by a gangly official who rose and shouted for the floor. The roar died down, and the stringy fellow, clad in russet velvet with the gold chain of the Master of the Seal about his neck, called out, "let the court find the traitor guilty summarily and put an end to this insupportable insolence..."

"Northroyal has been the victim of fraud," Retief said loudly in the comparative lull. "But not on my part. The man Rolan is an imposter."

CHAPTER EIGHT

A TERMENDOUS pounding of gavels and staffs eventually brought the outraged dignitaries to grim silence. The Presiding Justice peered down at Retief with doom in his lensed eyes. "Your knowledge of the Lilyan tongue and of the forms of court practice as well as the identity of your retinal patterns with those of the warrant tend to substantiate your origin in the Empire. Accordingly, this court is now disposed to recognize in you that basest of offenders, a renegade of the peerage." He raised his voice. "Let it be recorded that one Jame Jarl, a freelord of the Imperial Lily and officer Imperial of the Guard has by his own words disavowed his oath and his lineage." The fiery old man glared around at his fellow jurists. "Now let the dog of a broken officer be sentenced!"

"I have proof of what I say," Retief called out. "Nothing has been proven against me. I have acted by the Code, and by the Code I demand my hearing!"

"You have spurned the Code," said a fat dignitary.

"I have told you that a usurper sits on the Lily throne," Retief said. "If I can't prove it, execute me."

There was an icy silence.

"Very well," said the High Justice. "Present your proof."

"When the man, Rolan, appeared," Retief said, "he presented the Imperial seal and ring, the ceremonial robe, the major portion of the crown jewels, and the Imperial Genealogy."

"That is correct."

"Was it noted, by any chance, that the seal was without its chain, that the robe was stained, that the most important of the jewels, the ancient Napoleon Emerald, was missing; that the ring bore deep scratches, and that the lock on the book had been forced?"

A murmur grew along the high benches of the court. Intent eyes glared down at Retief.

"And was it not considered strange that the Imperial signet was not presented by this would-be Emperor, when that signet alone constitutes the true symbol of the Empire?" Retief's voice had risen to a thunderous loudness.

The High Justice stared now with a different emotion in his eyes.

"What do you know of these matters?" he demanded, but without assurance.

Retief reached into a tiny leather bag at his side and drew out something that he held out for inspection.

"This is a broken chain," he said. "It was cut when the seal was stolen from its place in Suite-in-Exile." He placed the heavy links on the narrow wainscot before him. "This," he said, "is the Napoleon Emerald, once worn by the legendary Bonaparte in a ring. It is unique in the galaxy, and easily proved genuine." There was utter stillness now. Retief placed a small key beside the chain and the gem. "This key will open the forced lock of the Imperial Genealogical Record."

Retief brought out an ornately wrought small silver casket and held it in view.

"The stains on the robe are the blood of the Emperor Ronare, shed by the knife of a murderer. The ring is scratched by the same knife, used to sever the finger in order to remove the ring," A murmur of horrified comment ran round the room now. Retief waited, letting all eyes focus on the silver box in his hand. It contained a really superb copy of the Imperial Signet; like the chain, the key and the emerald, the best that the science of the Corps could produce, accurate even in its internal molecular structure. It had to be, if it were to have a chance of acceptance. It would be put to the test without delay, matched to an electronic matrix with which it would, if acceptable, resonate perfectly. The copy had been assembled on the basis of some excellent graphic records; the original signet, as Retief knew, had been lost irretrievably in a catastrophic palace fire, a century and a half ago.

He opened the box, showed the magnificent wine-red crystal set in platinum. Now was the moment. "This is the talisman which alone would prove the falseness of the imposter Rolan," Retief said. "I call upon the honorable High Court to match it to the matrix; and while that is being done, I ask that the honorable Justices study carefully the genealogy included in the Imperial patent that I have presented to the court."

A messenger was dispatched to bring in the matrix while the Justices adjusted the focus of their corrective lenses and clustered over the document. The chamber buzzed with tense excitement. This was a fantastic development indeed!

The High Justice looked up as the massive matrix device was wheeled into the room. He stared at Retief. "This genealogy—" he began.

A Justice plucked at his sleeve, indicated the machine, whispering something. The High Justice nodded.

Retief handed the silver box down carefully to a page, watched as the chamber of the machine was opened, the great crystal placed in position. He held his breath as technicians twiddled controls, studied dials, then closed a switch. There was a sonorous musical tone from the machine.

The technician looked up.

"The crystal," he said, "does match the matrix."

Amid a burst of exclamations, which died as he faced the High Justice, Retief spoke.

"My lords, peers of the Imperial Lily," he said in a ringing voice, "know by this signet that we, Retief, by the grace of God Emperor, do now claim our rightful throne."

And just as quickly as the exclamations had died, they rose once more—a mixture of surprise and awe.

EPILOGUE

"A brilliant piece of work, Mr. Minister, and congratulations on your promotion," the Ambassador-at-large said warmly. "You've shown what individualism and the unorthodox approach can accomplish where the academic viewpoint would consider the situation hopeless."

"Thank you, Mr. Ambassador," Retief replied, smiling. "I was surprised myself when it was all over, that my gamble paid off. Frankly, I hope I won't ever be in a position again to be quite so inventive."

"I don't mind telling you now," the Ambassador said, "that when I saw Magnan's report of your solo assignment to the case, I seriously attempted to recall you, but it was too late. It was a nasty piece of business sending a single agent in on a job with the wide implications of this one. Mr. Magnan had been under a strain, I'm afraid. He is having a long rest now..."

Retief understood perfectly. His former chief had gotten the axe, and he himself had emerged clothed in virtue. That was the one compensation of desperate ventures; if you won, they paid well. In his new rank, he had a long tenure ahead. He hoped the next job would be something complex and far removed from Northroyal. He thought back over the crowded weeks of his brief reign there as Emperor. It had been a stormy scene when the bitterly resisting Rolan had been brought to face the High Court. The man had been hanged an hour before sunrise on the following day, still protesting his authenticity. That, at least, was a lie. Retief was grateful that he had proof that Rolan was a fraud, because he would have sent him to the gallows on false evidence even had he been the true heir.

His first act after his formal enthronement had been the abolition in perpetuity of the rite of the tourney, and the formal cancellation of all genealogical requirements for appointments public or private. He had ordered the release and promotion of the Battle Ensign who had ignored Rolan's arrest order and had been himself imprisoned for his pains. Fitzraven he had seen appointed to the Imperial War College—his future assured.

Retief smiled as he remembered the embarrassment of the young fellow who had been his fellow-finalist in the tourney. He had offered him satisfaction on the field of honor as soon as his arm healed, and had been asked in return for forgetfulness of poor judgment. He had made him a Captain of the Guard and a peer of the realm. He had the spirit for it.

There had been much more to do, and Retief's days had been crowded with the fantastically complex details of disengaging a social structure from the crippling reactionary restraints of ossified custom and hallowed tradition. In the end, he had produced a fresh and workable new constitution for the kingdom, which he hoped would set the world on an enlightened and dynamic path to a productive future.

THE MEMORY of Princess Monica lingered pleasantly; a true princess of the Lily, in the old tradition. Retief had abdicated in her favor; her genealogy had been studded with enough Imperial forebears to satisfy the crustiest of the Old Guard peerage; of course, it could not compare with the handsome document he had displayed showing his own descent in the direct line through seven— or was it eight—generations of Emperors-in-exile from the lost monarch of the beleaguered Lily Empire, but it was enough to justify his choice. Rolan's abortive usurpation had at least had the effect of making the Northroyalans appreciate an enlightened ruler.

At the last, it had not been easy to turn away forever from the seat of Empire that he so easily sat. It had not been lightly that he had said goodbye to the lovely Monica, who had reminded him of another dark beauty of long ago.

A few weeks in a modern hospital had remedied the harsher after-effects of his short career as a gladiator, and he was ready now for the next episode that fate and the Corps might have in store. But he would not soon forget Northroyal…

"…magnificent ingenuity," someone was saying. "You must have assimilated your indoctrination on the background unusually thoroughly to have been able to prepare in advance just those artifacts and documents that would prove most essential. And the technical skill in the production itself. Remarkable. To think that you were able to hoodwink the high priests of the cult in the very sanctum sanctorum."

"Merely the result of careful research," Retief said modestly. "I found all I needed on late developments, buried in our files. The making of the Signet was quite a piece of work; but credit for that goes to our own technicians."

"I was even more impressed by that document," a young counselor said. "What a knowledge of their psychology, and of technical detail that required."

Retief smiled faintly. The others had all gone into the hall now, amid a babble of conversation. It was time to be going. He glanced at the eager junior agent.

"No," he said, "I can't claim much credit there. I've had that document for many years; it, at least, was perfectly genuine."

THE END

If you've enjoyed this book, you will not want to miss these terrific titles…

ARMCHAIR SCI-FI & HORROR DOUBLE NOVELS, $12.95 each

D-1   **THE GALAXY RAIDERS** by William P. McGivern
SPACE STATION #1 by Frank Belknap Long

D-2   **THE PROGRAMMED PEOPLE** by Jack Sharkey
SLAVES OF THE CRYSTAL BRAIN by Rog Phillips

D-3   **YOU'RE ALL ALONE** by Fritz Leiber
THE LIQUID MAN by Bernard C. Gilford

D-4   **CITADEL OF THE STAR LORDS** by Edmond Hamilton
VOYAGE TO ETERNITY by Milton Lesser

D-5   **IRON MEN OF VENUS** by Don Wilcox
THE MAN WITH ABSOLUTE MOTION by Noel Loomis

D-6   **WHO SOWS THE WIND…** by Rog Phillips
THE PUZZLE PLANET by Robert A. W. Lowndes

D-7   **PLANET OF DREAD** by Murray Leinster
TWICE UPON A TIME by Charles L. Fontenay

D-8   **THE TERROR OUT OF SPACE** by Dwight V. Swain
QUEST OF THE GOLDEN APE by Paul W. Fairman & Milton Lesser

D-9   **SECRET OF MARRACOTT DEEP** by Henry Slesar
PAWN OF THE BLACK FLEET by Mark Clifton.

D-10   **BEYOND THE RINGS OF SATURN** by Robert Moore Williams
A MAN OBSESSED by Alan E. Nourse

ARMCHAIR SCIENCE FICTION CLASSICS, $12.95 each

C-1   **THE GREEN MAN**
by Harold M. Sherman

C-2   **A TRACE OF MEMORY**
By Keith Laumer

C-3   **INTO PLUTONIAN DEPTHS**
by Stanton A. Coblentz

ARMCHAIR MASTERS OF SCIENCE FICTION SERIES, $16.95 each

M-1   **MASTERS OF SCIENCE FICTION, Vol. One**
Bryce Walton—"Dark of the Moon" and other tales

M-2   **MASTERS OF SCIENCE FICTION, Vol. Two**
Jerome Bixby—"One Way Street" and other tales

If you've enjoyed this book, you will not want to miss these terrific titles...

ARMCHAIR SCI-FI & HORROR DOUBLE NOVELS, $12.95 each

D-11   **PERIL OF THE STARMEN** by Kris Neville
THE STRANGE INVASION by Murray Leinster

D-12   **THE STAR LORD** by Boyd Ellanby
CAPTIVES OF THE FLAME by Samuel R. Delany

D-13   **MEN OF THE MORNING STAR** by Edmond Hamilton
PLANET FOR PLUNDER by Hal Clement and Sam Merwin, Jr.

D-14   **ICE CITY OF THE GORGON** by Chester S. Geier and Richard Shaver
WHEN THE WORLD TOTTERED by Lester del Rey

D-15   **WORLDS WITHOUT END** by Clifford D. Simak
THE LAVENDER VINE OF DEATH by Don Wilcox

D-16   **SHADOW ON THE MOON** by Joe Gibson
ARMAGEDDON EARTH by Geoff St. Reynard

D-17   **THE GIRL WHO LOVED DEATH** by Paul W. Fairman
SLAVE PLANET by Laurence M. Janifer

D-18   **SECOND CHANCE** by J. F. Bone
MISSION TO A DISTANT STAR by Frank Belknap Long

D-19   **THE SYNDIC** by C. M. Kornbluth
FLIGHT TO FOREVER by Poul Anderson

D-20   **SOMEWHERE I'LL FIND YOU** by Milton Lesser
THE TIME ARMADA by Fox B. Holden

ARMCHAIR SCIENCE FICTION CLASSICS, $12.95 each

C-4   **CORPUS EARTHLING**
by Louis Charbonneau

C-5   **THE TIME DISSOLVER**
by Jerry Sohl

C-6   **WEST OF THE SUN**
by Edgar Pangborn

ARMCHAIR SCI-FI & HORROR GEMS SERIES, $12.95 each

G-1   **SCIENCE FICTION GEMS, Vol. One**
Isaac Asimov and others

G-2   **HORROR GEMS, Vol. One**
Carl Jacobi and others

If you've enjoyed this book, you will not want to miss these terrific titles…

ARMCHAIR SCI-FI & HORROR DOUBLE NOVELS, $12.95 each

D-21   **EMPIRE OF EVIL** by Robert Arnette
         THE SIGN OF THE TIGER by Alan E. Nourse & J. A. Meyer

D-22   **OPERATION SQUARE PEG** by Frank Belknap Long
         ENCHANTRESS OF VENUS by Leigh Brackett

D-23   **THE LIFE WATCH** by Lester del Rey
         CREATURES OF THE ABYSS by Murray Leinster

D-24   **LEGION OF LAZARUS** by Edmond Hamilton
         STAR HUNTER by Andre Norton

D-25   **EMPIRE OF WOMEN** by John Fletcher
         ONE OF OUR CITIES IS MISSING by Irving Cox

D-26   **THE WRONG SIDE OF PARADISE** by Raymond F. Jones
         THE INVOLUNTARY IMMORTALS by Rog Phillips

D-27   **EARTH QUARTER** by Damon Knight
         ENVOY TO NEW WORLDS by Keith Laumer

D-28   **SLAVES TO THE METAL HORDE** by Milton Lesser
         HUNTERS OUT OF TIME by Joseph E. Kelleam

D-29   **RX JUPITER SAVE US** by Ward Moore
         BEWARE THE USURPERS by Geoff St. Reynard

D-30   **SECRET OF THE SERPENT** by Don Wilcox
         CRUSADE ACROSS THE VOID by Dwight V. Swain

ARMCHAIR SCIENCE FICTION CLASSICS, $12.95 each

C-7   **THE SHAVER MYSTERY, Book One**
        by Richard S. Shaver

C-8   **THE SHAVER MYSTERY, Book Two**
        by Richard S. Shaver

C-9   **MURDER IN SPACE**
        by David V. Reed

ARMCHAIR MASTERS OF SCIENCE FICTION SERIES, $16.95 each

M-3   **MASTERS OF SCIENCE FICTION, Vol. Three**
        Robert Sheckley, "The Perfect Woman" and other tales

M-4   **MASTERS OF SCIENCE FICTION, Vol. Four**
        Mack Reynolds, Part One, "Stowaway" and other tales

If you've enjoyed this book, you will not want to miss these terrific titles...

ARMCHAIR SCI-FI & HORROR DOUBLE NOVELS, $12.95 each

D-31 **A HOAX IN TIME** by Keith Laumer
       INSIDE EARTH by Poul Anderson

D-32 **TERROR STATION** by Dwight V. Swain
       THE WEAPON FROM ETERNITY by Dwight V. Swain

D-33 **THE SHIP FROM INFINITY** by Edmond Hamilton
       TAKEOFF by C. M. Kornbluth

D-34 **THE METAL DOOM** by David H. Keller
       TWELVE TIMES ZERO by Howard Browne

D-35 **HUNTERS OUT OF SPACE** by Joseph Kelleam
       INVASION FROM THE DEEP by Paul W. Fairman,

D-36 **THE BEES OF DEATH** by Robert Moore Williams
       A PLAGUE OF PYTHONS by Frederik Pohl

D-37 **THE LORDS OF QUARMALL** by Fritz Leiber and Harry Fischer
       BEACON TO ELSEWHERE by James H. Schmitz

D-38 **BEYOND PLUTO** by John S. Campbell
       ARTERY OF FIRE by Thomas N. Scortia

D-39 **SPECIAL DELIVERY** by Kris Neville
       NO TIME FOR TOFFEE by Charles F. Meyers

D-40 **JUNGLE IN THE SKY** by Milton Lesser
       RECALLED TO LIFE by Robert Silverberg

ARMCHAIR SCIENCE FICTION CLASSICS, $12.95 each

C-10 **MARS IS MY DESTINATION**
       by Frank Belknap Long

C-11 **SPACE PLAGUE**
       by George O. Smith

C-12 **SO SHALL YE REAP**
       by Rog Phillips

ARMCHAIR SCI-FI & HORROR GEMS SERIES, $12.95 each

G-3 **SCIENCE FICTION GEMS, Vol. Two**
      James Blish and others

G-4 **HORROR GEMS, Vol. Two**
      Joseph Payne Brennan and others

If you've enjoyed this book, you will not want to miss these terrific titles...

ARMCHAIR SCI-FI & HORROR DOUBLE NOVELS, $12.95 each

D-41 **FULL CYCLE** by Clifford D. Simak
IT WAS THE DAY OF THE ROBOT by Frank Belknap Long

D-42 **THIS CROWDED EARTH** by Robert Bloch
REIGN OF THE TELEPUPPETS by Daniel Galouye

D-43 **THE CRISPIN AFFAIR** by Jack Sharkey
THE RED HELL OF JUPITER by Paul Ernst

D-44 **PLANET OF DREAD** by Dwight V. Swain
WE THE MACHINE by Gerald Vance

D-45 **THE STAR HUNTER** by Edmond Hamilton
THE ALIEN by Raymond F. Jones

D-46 **WORLD OF IF** by Rog Phillips
SLAVE RAIDERS FROM MERCURY by Don Wilcox

D-47 **THE ULTIMATE PERIL** by Robert Abernathy
PLANET OF SHAME by Bruce Elliot

D-48 **THE FLYING EYES** by J. Hunter Holly
SOME FABULOUS YONDER by Phillip Jose Farmer

D-49 **THE COSMIC BUNGLERS** by Geoff St. Reynard
THE BUTTONED SKY by Geoff St. Reynard

D-50 **TYRANTS OF TIME** by Milton Lesser
PARIAH PLANET by Murray Leinster

ARMCHAIR SCIENCE FICTION CLASSICS, $12.95 each

C-13 **SUNKEN WORLD**
by Stanton A. Coblentz

C-14 **THE LAST VIAL**
by Sam McClatchie, M. D.

C-15 **WE WHO SURVIVED (THE FIFTH ICE AGE)**
by Sterling Noel

ARMCHAIR MASTERS OF SCIENCE FICTION SERIES, $16.95 each

MS-5 **MASTERS OF SCIENCE FICTION, Vol. Five**
Winston K. Marks—Test Colony and other tales

MS-6 **MASTERS OF SCIENCE FICTION, Vol. Six**
Fritz Leiber—Deadly Moon and other tales

If you've enjoyed this book, you will not want to miss these terrific titles...

ARMCHAIR SCI-FI & HORROR DOUBLE NOVELS, $12.95 each

ARMCHAIR SCIENCE FICTION CLASSICS, $12.95 each

ARMCHAIR SCI-FI & HORROR GEMS SERIES, $12.95 each

If you've enjoyed this book, you will not want to miss these terrific titles…

ARMCHAIR SCI-FI & HORROR DOUBLE NOVELS, $12.95 each

D-61   **THE MAN WHO STOPPED AT NOTHING** by Paul W. Fairman
TEN FROM INFINITY by Ivar Jorgensen

D-62   **WORLDS WITHIN** by Rog Phillips
THE SLAVE by C.M. Kornbluth

D-63   **SECRET OF THE BLACK PLANET** by Milton Lesser
THE OUTCASTS OF SOLAR III by Emmett McDowell

D-64   **WEB OF THE WORLDS** by Harry Harrison and Katherine MacLean
RULE GOLDEN by Damon Knight

D-65   **TEN TO THE STARS** by Raymond Z. Gallun
THE CONQUERORS by David H. Keller, M. D.

D-66   **THE HORDE FROM INFINITY** by Dwight V. Swain
THE DAY THE EARTH FROZE by Gerald Hatch

D-67   **THE WAR OF THE WORLDS** by H. G. Wells
THE TIME MACHINE by H. G. Wells

D-68   **STARCOMBERS** by Edmond Hamilton
THE YEAR WHEN STARDUST FELL by Raymond F. Jones

D-69   **HOCUS-POCUS UNIVERSE** by Jack Williamson
QUEEN OF THE PANTHER WORLD by Berkeley Livingston

D-70   **BATTERING RAMS OF SPACE** by Don Wilcox
DOOMSDAY WING by George H. Smith

ARMCHAIR SCIENCE FICTION CLASSICS, $12.95 each

C-19   **EMPIRE OF JEGGA**
by David V. Reed

C-20   **THE TOMORROW PEOPLE**
by Judith Merril

C-21   **THE MAN FROM YESTERDAY**
by Howard Browne as by Lee Francis

C-22   **THE TIME TRADERS**
by Andre Norton

C-23   **ISLANDS OF SPACE**
by John W. Campbell

C-24   **THE GALAXY PRIMES**
by E. E. "Doc" Smith